The Queen's Corgi

The Queen's Corgi

On Purpose

A novel

DAVID MICHIE

First published in 2016
Copyright © Mosaic Reputation Management (Pty) Ltd 2016

Conch Books, an imprint of Mosaic Reputation Management (Pty) Ltd
Cover design: Margot Hutton
Author photo: Janmarie Michie
Proofreading: www.donnahillyer.com

Cataloguing-in-Publication details are available
from the National Library of Australia www.trove.nla.gov.au

ISBN 9780994488107
ISBN: 0994488106

In the tradition of David Michie's bestselling *The Dalai Lama's Cat* series, this charming, poignant and humorous novel about a dog's life with the royal family packs a deceptively powerful punch as it offers profound life lessons that will leave the reader transformed at a deeper level.

Ingrid King, award winning author of *Buckley's Story: Lessons from a Feline Master Teacher* and publisher of *The Conscious Cat.*

Narrated by a plucky pup of humble beginnings, *The Queen's Corgi* offer's a delightful dogs-eye-view of the most famous royal residence in the world. It's a tail-wagging treat to spend some quality time with Her Majesty and her best furry friend, a royal corgi whose wit and wisdom shine from beginning to end.

Julia Williams, CANIDAE RPO Blog Editor, www.canidae.com

Delightfully engaging and with an intriguing mystical flavour, this book not only entertains - it also takes us on a fascinating inner journey. David weaves in wise nuggets of wisdom which will make you stop, ponder and apply to your own life. Another glorious book from David Michie!

Tara Taylor, Intuitive Counselor, Motivational Speaker and Hay House Author of *Through Indigo's Eyes* series

Readers who fell in love with *The Dalai Lama's Cat,* the wise and shining feline star of the book series, have new cause for happiness: a charming new "rags to royalty" book by David Michie featuring a dog as the narrator. Not just any dog, but Nelson, an imperfect but witty corgi (with a large, furry ear for gossip and nose for misadventure) winds up as one of Queen of England's pack of Corgis and an all-access pass for behind-the-scenes palace life.

Layla Morgan Wilde, founder and editor of Cat Wisdom 101.com and producer of Cat Film Fest at Sea.

The Queen's Corgi captives from first page to last as the adorable puppy escapes death, and is carried into Windsor Castle to begin life as a royal corgi. David Michie's compelling writing style will keep you turning the pages of this heart-warming book with an understanding of dogs and the mysteries of life. Dog lovers of all ages will fall in love with *The Queen's Corgi*. Highly Recommended!

Darlene Arden, Certified Animal Behavior Consultant and author of *Small Dogs, Big Hearts: A Guide to Caring for your Little Dog*.

After a rough start in life, Nelson, the fictional corgi, gets to live with Queen Elizabeth II, soak in the wisdom of various famous folk, and have a winsome yet insightful book written for him by the inimitable David Michie. Talk about one lucky dog!

Michelle Fabio, writer and blogger at *BleedingEspresso*

Also by David Michie

Fiction
The Dalai Lama's Cat
The Dalai Lama's Cat and The Art of Purring
The Dalai Lama's Cat and The Power of Meow
The Magician of Lhasa

Non-fiction
Buddhism for Busy People
Hurry Up and Meditate
Enlightenment to Go
Why Mindfulness is Better than Chocolate

Dogs do speak, but only to those who know how to listen.

ORHAN PAMUK, *MY NAME IS RED*

Prologue

This book is being written by royal decree.

Well, sort of.

It all began on my favourite day of the year – the first of the Queen's annual summer visit to Balmoral Castle in Scotland. We three royal corgis were in a state of high excitement.

Having travelled up from Windsor with the household staff the previous day, we had arrived too late to see the Queen, who had already retired for the evening. Still closeted in a downstairs scullery when the family had left for church that morning, we were released just a few minutes before they were expected home.

The three of us romped through the ground floor, reacquainting ourselves with favourite suntraps and hidey-holes. We snuffled at the hearthrugs on which we had spent many a happy evening toasting ourselves before glowing log fires. We poked our snouts into half-forgotten corners, and raised them inquisitively towards the window, taking in the scents of gorse and heather, evocations of rambling country walks in summers past.

Winston, older than the Queen herself – albeit in dog years – headed with unusual haste towards the drawing room: the scene of his most tantalising discovery to date. It was behind a leather wing chair in the room, five years earlier, that he had come upon an overlooked and entirely uneaten plate of lobster vol-au-vents. He had devoured the snack in minutes. No matter how many unrewarded return visits he made to the room, whenever he turned in its direction the memory of that glorious find would light up his grizzled features.

Margaret, meantime, was trotting through the corridors, ears pointed and eyes alert. Her herding instincts stronger than most royal corgis, and her demand for service absolute, she was especially watchful of the staff. As every liveried helper in the royal household was painfully aware, the slightest infraction or delay could provoke a cautioning nip to the ankles.

I soon found my way to the large bay window in the dining room, and hopped up onto the broad, tartan-cushioned sill overlooking a corner of the garden. Twelve months before, that corner had been Football's favourite spot. Over the years I had struck up a special friendship with the large, marmalade cat who was a permanent resident of Balmoral. But scanning the landscape I could see no sign of him at present.

The sound of footmen and security heading towards the main entrance had all three of us racing from different parts of the castle as fast as our short legs would carry us. The front door was opened and from it we watched as the familiar convoy of cars approached the castle before slowing to a gracious stop. We scrambled down the short flight of steps. No matter which of the cars the Queen occupied, our canine instincts always led us unerringly to it.

You may very well wonder what it is like to find your-self in the presence of the Queen. Having seen a million of images of her on TV and in the papers, encountering her profile daily on banknotes, coins and postage stamps, it is only natural that you'd be curious to know how it feels to encounter one of the world's most famous people directly and in person.

Well, my fellow subject, let me enlighten you. When you meet the Queen, she is exactly as you would expect her to be – in appearance, at least. But she has another quality that catches most people by surprise. A quality which no television camera can capture and which few members of the media pack, corralled firmly behind ever-present railings, gets close enough to discover. You see, such is the Queen's sense of call-ing that, wherever she goes, she carries with her an almost-tangible expectation that your own deepest wish, like hers, is to serve a greater purpose.

To say that most people are caught unawares by this sen-sation would be an understatement. Expecting restrained and aloof, when they encounter Her Majesty's gentle but firm expectation of benevolence, they find themselves wishing – perhaps to their own surprise – to be the best that they can be. To act in accord with their highest ideals. I have witnessed many people who are so taken aback by this unspoken appeal to their own better natures that they're quite overcome with emotion.

'Hello, my little ones!' the Queen greeted us that day as she emerged from the car. Winston and Margaret were red and white Pembrokes, while I had the distinction of a sable-coloured saddle on my back. All three of us rushed about her ankles, our tail stubs wagging frenziedly. We were as delighted to feel her gloved hands patting our necks as she seemed thrilled to see us after more than 24 hours apart.

Soon the whole family was heading inside.

'Very nice service,' the Queen remarked as they made their way to the drawing room.

'Kenneth always has something sensible to say,' agreed Camilla.

'Outside the church was a bit worrying,' observed Charles. 'How many journalists?' Tugging at his earlobe, he used much the same tone of voice as if querying a troubling aphid infestation at his rose garden at Highgrove.

'Twice as many as last year,' said William.

'The numbers are growing.' The Queen was apprehensive.

One of the reasons she so enjoyed these visits to Scotland was the opportunity to get away from the constant prying of telephoto lenses and long-range microphones.

As Her Majesty settled on a sofa, Philip eased himself down gingerly beside her. He looked over at her, with a fiercely protective expression, lips quivering.

'Bloody journalists!' he said.

'One of them called out to Kate wanting an interview,' announced William.

'The nerve!' harrumphed Charles. The church in nearby Crathie had traditionally been a photo opportunity-only venue, with journalists expected to keep their distance.

As the rest of the family sat down, the household staff brought in tea and scones.

'Well, I shan't let them spoil my holiday,' declared Anne. 'I shall simply ignore them.'

The expressions of the others suggested that this was advice they found difficult to follow.

'They won't go away, Gran.' Unlike the other family members, Harry was sitting on the floor massaging Margaret's ears as she gazed at him beatifically. 'Unless,' he continued, 'you give them something.'

The Queen, like Margaret, had always had a soft spot for Harry, valuing him as a direct conduit to the younger generation. 'What might that be?' she asked.

He shrugged. 'Not sure. We'd have to come up with something.'

Kate was nodding. 'Something safe and light-hearted. Something summer-y.'

'Like who designed your T-shirt?' joked William.

'And,' she responded, 'whether it was … Made in Britain?' The last three words were chorused by all the younger royals, having learned, to their cost, the furore that would accompany their purchase of items that weren't manufactured in the UK – or a Commonwealth country at least.

'Such a pity the media insist on running page after page of drivel,' Charles repeated his oft-made observation. 'Wouldn't it be wonderful if newspapers did more to share stories and insights that were really meaningful? Things that might help people lead more purposeful lives.'

The Queen glanced over at him, uncertainly. 'Tricky business, persuading the media to lift their sights from terror and trivia. Every one of us has tried.'

Pushing myself up so that I was balancing on my rear end, I fixed Kate with a pleading expression. She was a soft touch when it came to scones.

There was a pause while the family glanced in my direction. Before Kate said, 'Well, not *every* family member.'

'Genius!' congratulated Harry. Then, responding to the bafflement of the older royals, 'We offer the media a story about the royal corgis. Videos and photos. A few words about their personalities. Then they can skedaddle for the summer, leaving us in peace.'

William raised an eyebrow. 'Worth a try.'

'We might even get one of the corgis to say something meaningful,' joked Harry, trying to win his father around.

'I'm sure Winston would have a great deal to say if he didn't get sidetracked,' replied Charles drolly.

Harry pulled a face, and, in a stage whisper, said, 'Vol-au-vents!'

The family laughed.

'You can forget Margaret,' said Anne. 'Given half a chance she'd leave them all bleeding at the ankles.'

At this point Her Majesty, who had yet to comment on the idea, observed, 'It would have to be Nelson. He has always been the most diplomatic of the corgis.'

Realising that my attempt to coax a scone out of Duchess Kate was futile – she was not going to do so in front of the Queen – I dropped to the floor and made my way over to Her Majesty.

'Perhaps you could say something meaningful on our behalf? Something about purpose?' the Queen enquired looking directly at me.

'After the life he's led,' observed Kate, 'he could write a whole book.'

'Splendid idea,' the Queen replied, smiling. '*The Queen's Corgi*! One would be most interested to read it.'

And so, in a metaphorical sense, the ball was thrown.

Mulling over the conversation in the glorious days that followed, I began to realize just how true Kate's observation was. It was a rare week when I didn't come nose to ankle – if not snout to groin – with the most famous people in show-biz, arts, sports and spirituality. There were few of the world's most pre-eminent politicians, pop stars or philosophers who weren't, at some point, ushered into the royal presence. I had sniffed them all, even peed on a few, but let's not spoil this first chapter by bringing dog-eating despots into it.

Not only had I met a richly varied and colourful range of human beings, along with a great many bores, I had also been witness to extraordinary encounters that most people will never see. I had eavesdropped on intriguing insights from the highest-level advisers, the best of the best, with whom Her Majesty consults.

What's more, it struck me that the never-ending flow of TV and press coverage, films and books about the royal family had one singular thing in common – they were all from a human perspective. Where was the dog's-eye view? The under-the-table account? What people discovered about the Queen, from the perspective of her most diplomatic of Pembroke Welsh Corgis would, I had no doubt at all, prove refreshingly different.

So here we are, you and me embarking on this journey to-gether. One filled with intriguing aromas, wagging tail stumps and something else I am supposed to remember. What was it again? Ah, yes – purpose.

What's the point of it all, people sometimes ask? The crowns and castles. The pomp and circumstance. Why both-er? Who cares? How can the royal family possibly add to the sum of human happiness – and, let's not forget, canine, feline and other -ine happiness too?

Perhaps the answers to some of those questions will be revealed in the pages that follow.

Perhaps not.

But one thing I am sure of, my fellow subject: it is not by chance that you hold this book in your hands.

One

From my earliest days I was aware of a place called 'the shed'. To begin with I had no idea where it was. But on the very rare occasions that the Grimsleys paid me any attention, 'the shed' was invoked. And even as a puppy only a few weeks old, I knew instinctively that it was a place where terrible things happened.

I was born into the most humble of circumstances, under the kitchen sink in a cramped terraced house in Slough. The youngest in a litter of five pups, and very much smaller than the others, I soon found myself competing for space and attention not only with my immediate brothers and sisters, who shared a sack in the carcass of what used to be a kitchen cupboard, but also with two older and sturdier litters belonging to other mothers in the house. There were over twenty of us in all.

It was not an even competition. My size counted against me, as did my right ear which, instead of standing, flopped. Desperate for the same affection the Grimsleys bestowed on the other pups, it seemed that my dysfunctional ear rendered me unloveable.

In the rough and ready chaos of discarded pizza boxes and crushed cans of Fosters beer, dirty laundry and the

1

ever-present, pungent aroma of kipper, the house was completely given over to corgis. We were everywhere: under the kitchen bench, where cupboard doors had been removed to create kennels; nesting behind sitting room sofas; suckling and scratching under the Grimsleys' bed.

On the rare occasion I came to the attention of Mrs Grimsley, she'd jab her cigarette towards me in distaste. 'Still not standing,' she'd say with a sigh, exhaling a stream of acrid smoke.

Mr Grimsley, a very large man in worn, denim overalls with watery blue eyes, would stare at me in slack-jawed silence.

'You're going to have to take it down the shed,' Mrs Grimsley would instruct.

'Give it time,' Mr Grimsley might say. 'Perhaps he's a late bloomer.'

'That's always been your problem, Reg.' Mrs Grimsley's voice was brittle. 'Too soft. Waste of Kibbles, that one.'

None of the corgis knew exactly what happened in the shed. Other dogs were said to have been taken there in the past – all of them stunted in some way. The only thing known for certain was that once a corgi went to the shed, it was never seen again.

On Saturday mornings, the Grimsleys would be transformed, Mr Grimsley appearing downstairs first, having squeezed uncomfortably into a dark suit, followed by pencil-thin Mrs Grimsley, all blonde hair and red lipstick, talking in her Kennel Club voice.

'Are Tarquin and Annabelle in the car?' she'd want to know. 'In their show collars? Where's Tudor's pedigree?'

A lengthy and restive day indoors for all the dogs would be followed by an even-lengthier evening waiting for the Grimsleys to get home from whichever home county they had visited, usually followed by a lock-in at the local pub, The Crown. Being small and vulnerable, I usually avoided the scamper and tumble of the other corgis, only venturing far from the kitchen cupboard in the reassuring presence of my eldest brother, Jasper.

'Hurry up, Number Five.' He'd cock his head playfully, trying to coax me out; I was the only corgi in the house that had no name. 'There's a whole week's laundry to get our teeth into!'

In the early hours of a Sunday morning, Mrs Grimsley would lurch through the front door, Mr Grimsley stumbling after her in his great, dark, tent of a suit, and Tarquin and Annabelle plodding behind, exhausted by a day trapped in cage and car.

'Don't you just love corgis?!' Mrs Grimsley would slump into a chair, grabbing banknotes out of her handbag and tossing them up in the air so that they fluttered, confetti-like, all around her. 'Eight hundred pounds! And another seven pups as good as sold. Oh, Annabelle, my little darling!' she'd croon in a way that she never did for me. 'What a wonder you are!'

One by one, as the older pups reached a certain age, they were taken out to meet their new owners in the nearby park. The Grimsleys avoided having buyers to their home, the front door being hard to access on account of the two Morris Minors rusting on bricks in the driveway. They had been a decaying fixture for as long as anyone knew, awaiting the day that Mr Grimsley began to restore them to classic glory.

On the rare occasion that a visitor unavoidably came to the house, I was hastily shut in the upstairs box room. 'Ruin our reputation, it would,' Mrs Grimsley used to declare, 'having this one seen with its ear. We can't having people thinking we breed bitsas.'

There could be no harsher condemnation than for a dog than to be described as a 'bitsa', as the Grimsleys referred to dogs of uncertain breeding – a bit of this and a bit of that.

As the weeks passed, Mrs Grimsley took more and more of the older dogs to the park, returning alone, an unused lead wrapped around one hand, and bulging wallet in the other. Then my own immediate brothers and sisters began to be sold off. The once-cramped conditions under the kitchen sink became strangely spacious, the reassuring crush of bodies less dense.

As I became more and more visible, I was the focus of the same, sinister conversation. Mrs Grimsley's demand that I be taken to the shed became increasingly shrill. Mr Grimsley dropped all talk of me being a late bloomer.

'I'll see to it,' he'd promise her, darkly.

One day I turned to Jasper and asked what Mr Grimsley meant.

'Hard to guess, Number Five, but I wouldn't worry about it.' He looked away. 'According to our mother, he's been saying he'll see to the two Morris Minors since the time of our great-grandparents.'

I knew Jasper was trying to be reassuring. But I could sense his disquiet.

And Mrs Grimsley wasn't letting go. Things reached an all-time low the afternoon that she returned alone from having taken Jasper himself to the park, with the rolled-up lead in one hand and an envelope in the other. I realised what had happened but still stared foolishly at the front door as though I could somehow will my big brother back to the house. Eventually I looked up. Mrs Grimsley was staring at me with an expression of cold determination.

'It's no good, Reg!' She shouted to her husband, who was coming down the stairs. 'You're going to have to take it down the shed.'

'But –'

'Gone on long enough.' She was insistent. 'Today!'

'I'm just on my way out –'

'Right now.'

'Alright.' He flapped his heavy arms in surrender. 'Alright. When I get back from The Crown.'

'I'll hold you do it.'

'I'll see to it then.'

Returning to the cupboard under the kitchen sink, I slumped down in a state of abject misery. Even though it was hard being a stunted, unloved corgi in a house filled with bright-eyed pedigrees who were lavished with affection, I preferred staying where I was than to having to face the unknown horror at the bottom of the garden.

Mrs Grimsley was watching *Eastenders* in the front room when the there was a knocking at the door.

'Who is it?' she called from the hallway.

'I've come about a corgi!' A woman's voice sounded clear and authoritative.

'Hang on a minute.'

Finding me in the kitchen, Mrs Grimsley closed the door firmly before going to greet her visitor.

'I hear you may have a puppy for sale –'

'All gone,' interrupted Mrs Grimsley briskly. 'I can put you on the waiting list. We're expecting a litter next month.'

'This particular puppy,' said the other woman, 'has a floppy ear.'

There was a pause while Mrs Grimsley inhaled.

'Don't know where you heard that,' she pronounced smokily. 'The pedigree of our corgis is impeccable.'

'I'm quite sure it is.' The other woman seemed altogether unruffled by her reaction.

'We don't breed duds,' insisted Mrs Grimsley.

'A floppy ear is only a problem if you plan to show. We have no such plans.'

'Don't know where this tittle tattle comes from.'

'Mr Grimsley, actually. At The Crown.'

'The bloody idiot!' screeched Mrs Grimsley in a voice that was definitely not Kennel Club.

'Look.' The other woman's voice was firm. 'I'll pay you a thousand pounds for him.'

The pause that followed didn't last very long before I heard the sound of approaching footsteps. The kitchen door being opened. For the first time since I was a very new puppy, Mrs Grimsley picked me up. 'He's actually our little favourite,' she crooned in a voice she'd never used before with me – the one she only adopted when cuddling her favourites. As she turned, I found myself looking into the kindly face of a very beautiful woman in her late thirties. I pricked up my ears – well, the left one, and half of the right.

'Good.' The woman reached into her handbag and retrieved a clip of crisp, new banknotes, which she held out.

Mrs Grimsley looked at the notes only briefly before taking them in her right hand, and thrusting me into the visitor's arms.

'Promise not to say where you got him,' she demanded, in her smoker's voice.

'Fine.'

'I never want to hear of him again.'

'You won't.'

I immediately felt safe in the arms of the visitor. As she held me to her chest in a manner that suggested she was used to holding dogs, along with a faint scent of lavender I sensed a calm reassurance that couldn't be more different to Mrs Grimsley.

'If you mention me –' Mrs Grimsley was following us out of the house '– I'll deny all knowledge. I'll say you're a lying toerag.'

'Oh, you needn't trouble yourself on that score, Mrs Grimsley,' said the woman, stepping across the short front yard and into the street. 'I'm quite happy to forget that we ever met.'

The drive from the Grimsleys' terrace house in Slough to Windsor Castle wasn't a long one. Fewer than twenty minutes in the car separated what was to become my new life from my old. But even though I was in a dog carrier in the back of a car – both unfamiliar experiences – driven by a woman who was a complete stranger, I felt a powerful sense of relief; compared to being taken down to the shed, it couldn't be as bad.

Could it?

I won't pretend to remember much of my first arrival at Windsor Castle. In the twilight it was all a confusion of gates and security checks and dark passages smelling of beeswax until, all of a sudden, I was in a spacious, red-carpeted hallway, hung with paintings and lit by chandeliers. My rescuer, who I discovered was called Lady Tara, the Queen's lady-in-waiting, walked purposefully along the hallway, with me still in the carrier, before making her way up a staircase.

This was nothing like the stairs I was used to. Not only were they very much wider and more luxuriously carpeted, there was not a single pile of unwashed laundry, nor even a crushed beer can to be seen. Nor was there the faintest tang of kipper. My first impression of the castle was also how vast the rooms were. And how empty of corgis.

I was suddenly somewhat startled by a soldier, armoured in ancient chain mail, who was standing at attention on the staircase landing. And somewhat surprised that Tara completely ignored him, brushing past him as if he wasn't there.

After walking along another broad corridor, similarly void of dogs, Tara took me into a suite of rooms before coming to a door that was slightly ajar. Reaching into the carrier, she lifted me out, before knocking gently.

We walked across a very large room, at the other side of which a short, silver-haired woman was working at her desk. The room had dark, wood-panelled walls, the only light coming from a desk lamp, which glowed warmly, illuminating the woman's features. Even at first glance, my fellow subject, I knew there was something different about her. Something that set her apart. It didn't have to do with her appearance so much as an invisible – but no less tangible – sense of presence.

As soon as she saw us approaching, she rose to her feet.

'So, this is him?' she asked, coming to meet us.

'Yes ma'am.'

Him, I noted, not the *it* by which Mrs Grimsley had always referred to me.

Stepping closer, the lady I would soon learn was the Queen beamed as she reached out to stroke my head. 'Handsome little chap. Beautiful markings.'

I responded to her attention by pricking up one and a half ears.

'Oh, I see. Gives him such character, don't you think?'

Too young to understand exactly what she meant, I knew from her tone of voice that the Queen seemed to be saying that my floppy ear was a *good* thing. What an utterly amazing and wonderful idea! I was immediately licking her hand.

She chuckled. 'Friendly little fellow.'

'Hard to believe what they were planning to do to him,' observed Tara.

'Yes, but we shouldn't judge,' replied the Queen. 'Not everyone enjoys our circumstances.'

In the pause that followed I wondered what those plans had been, beyond my being taken to the shed. It would be months before I discovered the full story and how, the moment that Tara told Her Majesty about my impending fate at the hands of Mr Grimsley, she had been dispatched to rescue me.

'I'm sure he's going to settle in very well,' said the Queen.

'Would you like me to take him down to join the others?'

'He's probably had enough to deal with for one day. He can stay with me tonight,' Her Majesty said with a nod, before turning back towards her desk.

It took me a while to realise that I had a new home. A permanent one. It seemed quite surreal that instead of the kitchen cupboard, I had been transported to this strange place with its empty rooms and not a whiff of cigarette smoke, much less stale beer.

Taking me to the private sitting room next door, Tara produced a bowl of food more delicious than even the finest the Grimsleys used to serve to their champion pedigrees. I wolfed it down in short order, and took a few laps of water. A very comfortable basket was brought for me to sleep in. I gathered that the sitting room was where I was to remain for the time being.

My feelings about this new place were strangely mixed. My initial relief was soon followed by acute loneliness – for the first time in my life I was without a very large and extended family, and, most especially, without Jasper. As a very small, underdeveloped pup, on my very first night away from home, I wished I could be back in familiar surroundings –without the threat of the shed, of course.

Tara looked in on me several times that evening, always dependably comforting, as did several men I came to know, both individually and collectively, as 'security'.

Nevertheless, I was feeling quite bereft by the time I heard the Queen saying goodnight to a man called Philip. As soon as she came through the door, I jumped out of my basket and hurried over to her, tail stump wagging. She bent down and made a great fuss of me, before coming over to pick up the basket, which she took through to her bedroom, placing it near the side of her bed.

I watched her return later in her bedclothes. Sitting up against the pillows she closed her eyes, and for quite some time remained silent.

Her Majesty, I soon came to realise, is a deeply spiritual person. Not in a way that feels the need to be voiced, but one, rather, that is implicit in her actions. Not in a narrow, exclusive sense, but founded on personal experience of our own true nature, one that goes well beyond the limits of ordinary conception.

By the time she switched off the light, a peacefulness had descended not only on her, but on the whole room.

'Welcome to Windsor, little one,' she whispered in the dark, to reassure me. 'And goodnight.'

The reassurance worked.

For a while.

Then the pitch blackness of the room, the unfamiliar sounds echoing through the castle corridors, the lack of half a dozen other corgis pressed close to me under the kitchen sink, and the absence of the pong of kipper, made me feel somehow alone and adrift.

I whimpered.

The Queen shushed me.

I was quiet for a while. Before I whimpered again.

'We can't have this,' said the Queen, getting out of bed, and lifting me up on top of it.

Back at the Grimsleys, only the champion pedigrees used to sleep with the humans. And even though at that point I had no idea who Her Majesty was, I still realised I was being accorded a very special privilege.

Snuggling close, I thought how it was through her doing that I had been rescued from the Grimsleys. How it was she who was giving me a new home. How she cared for me even though I had a floppy ear – perhaps even because of it. Gratitude surging through me, and I showed my love in the way that we dogs know best: I licked her face.

'Oh, no!' she chuckled, wriggling away.

Thinking she wanted to play, I wriggled after her.

'If this carries on –' her tone had changed '– I'll have to take you downstairs.'

Downstairs was not a place I had any wish to be, so, instead, I settled halfway down the bed. Which was how, my fellow subject, on my first night away from under the Grimsleys' kitchen sink, I slept with the Queen of the United Kingdom.

In the days that followed I learned more about the world than I could ever have imagined. I was fortunate to have as my mentor, the life-long and most faithful companion to the Queen, Winston. I met him and Margaret on my very first morning when we were all fed breakfast in the staff kitchen, where the royal corgis were traditionally fed, and from which we were allowed into the staff garden to answer the call of nature. As it happened, my naivety about royal protocol served me well. Coming from a house full of corgis, as soon as I saw them I wasted no time in introducing myself by sniffing their backsides, my tail stump wagging vigorously.

Margaret, who had no time for stand-offish blue-bloods who thought rather a lot of themselves, decided on that first meeting that I was a corgi she could do business with. Winston, at the advanced age of twelve, saw in me a younger version of himself and had soon adopted me as his protégé.

It was he who patiently explained the facts of my new life.

'Strange name for a person, "The Queen",' I observed that first morning at Windsor Castle.

'It's not a name, it's a title,' he corrected me. Having started the day with a hearty breakfast of biscuits, the two of us
were snuffling round our breakfast bowls in the hope of finding a displaced morsel.

'Title.' I pondered for a bit. 'You mean like "Champion
Pedigree"?'

'Indeed.' Discovering a fragment of biscuit near the
skirting board, Winston had quickly licked it into his
mouth and was crunching with immense satisfaction. 'The
Queen is the pre-eminent of all champion pedigrees. She is
a direct descendent of William the Conqueror – 1066 and
all that.'

I didn't know what he meant exactly. Or, even, at all. And
a pedigree of a thousand years was quite beyond my comprehension. Up till then I had no idea that pedigrees applied to
humans, but Winston assured me that they did. My rescuer
Tara was a blue blood, he explained, because she had 'Lady'
in front of her name. Thinking about the Grimsleys, I came
to realise how they were almost certainly 'bitsas' – an idea that
made my head spin.

'Does the Queen have a real name?' I continued to parade
my ignorance that first morning.

'It's "Elizabeth",' he said, 'but no one outside the family
has actually called her that since she became Queen. Well,
there was one person.'

I looked at him enquiringly.

'That African fellow. Margaret –' he looked up to where
she sat, ears alert, watching the sous chef whose job it was to
feed us '– what's the name of that African president, the one
who was overly familiar.'

'Who?' She pretended not to have been listening. I could tell she was just being officious and knew exactly who he was talking about.

'The one with the loud shirts,' he continued.

'Nelson Mandela.'

'That's him. He called her Elizabeth. Don't think she minded so much in his case.'

My mind was bursting with questions. 'Apart from having a title is she just like other humans?'

Winston snorted. I came to know that this most Winstonian of characteristics – somewhere between a sigh and a cough – could mean any number of things: surprise, amusement, outrage or, as at the moment, a combination of world weariness with a sense of profound wisdom.

'She is and she isn't,' he answered after a while.

I was to learn that Winston sometimes spoke in riddles. He was the kind of dog happy to point you in a particular direction, but who preferred you to work things out for yourself.

'She has a human body, but she was born into extraordinary position and power. You don't think that happened by chance, do you?'

The truth of the matter was that I hadn't thought about it at all. The idea of being a Queen was an entirely new concept to me.

'She is by far the best informed person in Britain.' Margaret glanced across as the sous chef made his way out of the room. 'For over sixty years she has been regularly briefed by intelligence agencies, the military, bankers, prime ministers … the most powerful people in the land.'

'Since time immemorial her family have been the knowledge holders of all the esoteric traditions of Celtic culture

–' a far-away look came into Winston's eye '– handed down through the generations. At the top end of a fishbowl, everyone knows all the concepts. Some embody the dark, and others the light.'

'How do you mean?'

'These things,' he said mysteriously, 'are better seen than explained. Keep your wits about you. Look sharp.'

There was a pause while I digested both my breakfast as well as the intriguing reality in which I had found myself.

There was another question I just had to ask. 'Why all the red carpets?'

'Why indeed,' intoned Winston.

'Red is the colour of royalty.' Margaret was matter-of-fact. 'Of strength and power.'

'It is also the symbol of bloodlines and lineage,' observed Winston.

'Champion pedigrees?' I confirmed.

'Yes.' He regarded me closely, scrutinising my features as though trying to make up his mind about something, before finally saying, 'For those who embody the esoteric path, the same energies may return to the same bloodlines.'

This was a great deal for a corgi new to the household – and a pup at that – to try to understand.

'Well,' I mused after a while, 'does all this mean that are we unlike other corgis?'

'Of course!' exclaimed Margaret. 'We are Her Majesty's representatives.'

'Ours is not so much a position,' intoned Winston, 'as a sacred duty. World without end.'

'Amen.' Margaret, finished off, with a lick of the lips.

Winston and Margaret explained that even though we were the Queen's corgis, I shouldn't expect to spend much time with her every day. A relentless calendar of activity meant that for much of the year she had little time to herself. But she would try to include us in as many of her activities as possible.

As it happened, that very first morning we were with Her Majesty when she received a visitor – my first witness of a royal audience. I watched in fascination as Lord Cranleigh entered the room and approached where the Queen was standing, the three of us at her feet. Margaret bared her teeth ever so slightly as the large, tall, silvering man in the dark suit came closer, before bowing very deeply.

'How do you do?' The Queen extended her hand for the briefest handshake, before gesturing towards a chair.

The two of them sat, joined by the sovereign's private secretary, a genial man called Julian. Tea was brought in, and a discussion followed about Her Majesty's forthcoming visit to the Lake District.

Taking my cue from Winston and Margaret, I lay down on a nearby oriental carpet of great antiquity. While the two other corgis dozed through what, for them, was just another day at the office, I rested my face between my front paws and watched the Queen intently.

Something about the atmosphere of the room – of the whole castle – felt special and otherworldly. Later I was to discover that it was the oldest and longest-occupied castle in Europe. Its history was almost tangible, along with the design of this room with its very high ceilings, tall windows and sumptuous fittings. A very large chamber lit only by the light of the window, and picture lamps that blazed above large, gilt-framed oil paintings of the Queen's ancestors, there was the sense of being in an inner sanctum, a place from which you could experience an unusually rarefied view of the world. In time I came to know that the feeling didn't actually come from castle or its fittings – it came from the presence of Her Majesty. And it was a presence she encouraged others to share.

I discovered this for myself on that very first morning when conversation took a sudden turn in my direction. Arrangements for the Lake District having been duly discussed, the Queen rose to her feet, thus signalling to Lord Cranleigh that his audience was over. As the two men made their way to the door, the Queen stood. Winston and Margaret roused themselves and went to see them off. I followed.

'Ah – a third corgi!' observed Lord Cranleigh.

Julian glanced in my direction. 'Joined us only last night.'

'The ear,' the Lord murmured under his breath as the two men reached the door.

'What's that?' Her Majesty's hearing was much more acute than many imagined.

'I was just saying ...' Lord Cranleigh turned, struggling to find the right form of words '... your new corgi's ear ...'

'Yes?'

'Well, it's not sort of ... it isn't entirely ... the way it's presenting ...'

'It flops.'

'Yes, ma'am.'

'What of it?'

'Well, it's just that all your other dogs being normal, I'm a bit ... surprised.'

'His hearing is just as good as the others. He's quite normal.'

'Quite so, ma'am,' Lord Cranleigh agreed very quickly.

'Being young, he's in need of reassurance.' The Queen took a few steps towards where the men were standing. 'If we want him to grow up happy and well adjusted, he needs our affection and support. *That's* what really matters.' She spoke deliberately. 'Wouldn't you agree, Lord Cranleigh?'

'Of course, ma'am. Without question.'

'It's important not to get sidetracked by the superficial.'

'No, ma'am.'

'When we make judgements about things based on appearance, instead of on what really matters, we get into trouble.' She was holding Lord Cranleigh's eyes firmly, but not without warmth. 'Our own well-being and the well-being of those around us depends on being guided by the right priorities, wouldn't you agree?'

'Absolutely, ma'am. Quite so.'

Julian ushered Lord Cranleigh out of the room and we three corgis made our way back to the Queen.

Winston sidled up to me. 'That wasn't about you, by the way.'

'No?'

'Her Majesty is always well briefed about visitors.'

'It sounded like it was about me.' I was bewildered.

'All in good time,' he said, enigmatically. 'Look sharp.'

Early that evening there was an award ceremony for The Prince's Trust in the Waterloo Chamber – a room usually closed to the public, Margaret told me, as we accompanied Sophia from the Queen's quarters to the chamber.

Sophia shared an office with the Queen's lady-in-waiting, and helped arrange the charitable engagements of senior members of the royal family. While Tara, the epitome of English beauty, was always immaculately dressed with perfectly coiffed blonde hair and an aura of calm self-assurance, Sophia, a few years younger, was more vivacious and impulsive. Her dark good looks and high spirits livened up the atmosphere at the palace, and it was clear that the two women enjoyed a warm friendship.

There was something enigmatic about Tara, however, which Sophia saw as her job to resolve: the absence of a boyfriend. Despite being showered with invitations to social events every night of the week, apparently, for some reason, whenever Tara became involved with an eligible man, the relationship never lasted.

As soon as Sophia announced she was going to the Waterloo Chamber, Winston had sprung from where he'd been dozing beside her desk.

'Winston is very keen on award ceremonies,' I observed to Margaret as the two of us followed.

'Not the ceremony. It's what happens afterwards. Young ones always think they're being very daring when they sneak canapés to the Queen's corgis. Winston takes full advantage.'

The Waterloo Chamber was magnificent, a huge wood-panelled room with an ornate, vaulted ceiling, red-and-gold carpets and massive oil paintings in gilded frames. A steady stream of visitors were pouring in, young men awkward in suits and ties, and young women teetering on heels evidently bought especially for the occasion. Glancing about, they seemed overawed by the majesty of the place as they were guided towards rows of chairs.

For my own part, it was my first, public appearance as a Queen's corgi – one for which I was entirely unprepared. From having been the very least important dog in a house of over twenty, and painfully aware of my inadequacies, suddenly I felt very special. There was a ripple of excitement as soon as people saw the three of us strutting across the carpet. Many smiled and pointed. Others tried to coax us to them. From being an outcast only the day before, about to be taken to the terrifying fate of whatever awaited me in the shed, suddenly I was a star! 'We are Her Majesty's representatives,' Margaret had said. Now I understood exactly what she meant! The simple fact of our presence made people feel closer to the Queen herself, giving them the sense that she might step into the room at any moment.

I kept hard on the heels of Sophia and, along with Winston and Margaret, sat next to her in the front row of seats, near a small stage on which several council members of The Prince's Trust faced the audience. They were, Margaret told me approvingly, all highly successful businessmen.

One of them, a bouncy looking man with a mane of silver hair, was soon opening proceedings by introducing, as a VIP guest, a leading expert on happiness.

'Oh, spare us!' snorted Winston. 'A speaker.'

'I'd like to congratulate every single one of you who is here this evening,' began the visiting expert, a friendly-looking man with short, dark hair and glinting spectacles, who spoke with what I later discovered to be an Australian accent.

'Each one of you has not only found your way out of unemployment, but you have completely turned your lives around. Tonight is a celebration of that achievement.'

Several Prince's Trust committee members applauded enthusiastically.

'What I'm here to talk about this evening is the more important question underlying what we all do. It's a question each one of us has to answer in his or her own particular way. But there are some common threads. The question I am talking about is: how can we lead happy and purposeful lives?'

From the silence in the room, the speaker evidently had everyone's attention.

'The ancient Greeks didn't have just one word for happiness, they had two: *hedonia* and *eudemonia*. It's unfortunate that, in everyday English, we no longer make the same distinction because there's an important difference. *Hedonia* is happiness we get when we take *from* the world. Chocolate. Parties. Stuff. It's all coming from outside ourselves.

'*Eudemonia*, on the other hand, is the happiness we get from what we give *to* the world. The concern we show for others when we offer our time, skills, support. It's a different quality of happiness that comes from within.'

The VIP expert went on to talk about how the two kinds of happiness differ. How *hedonia* focuses on me and the pleasure I get. How the focus of *eudemonia* is on others, and the happiness we experience from helping them. How *hedonia* tends to be short-lived, and the more we experience it, the less it delivers. 'The first slice of cake is one thing,' he observed. 'How about the second, the fifth, the tenth?'

At Sophia's feet, Winston was fidgeting. 'Amateur!' he snuffled. 'But I take his point.'

By contrast, the inner contentment of *eudemonia* is more enduring, the speaker noted. And that feeling is not diminished by repetition. If anything, the more we keep giving, the more profound our sense of well-being.

I found the visiting expert's talk very interesting. Enlightening, even. I had never heard such ideas expressed in the time I'd been growing up in the Grimsley household. The lives of Mr and Mrs Grimsley, it was plain to see, were given over completely to *hedonia*. Hardly surprising, therefore, that they were often so miserable, and the only solace they seemed to find was an altered state of consciousness courtesy of The Crown.

'Go for both!' urged the speaker at his conclusion. 'Enjoy the pleasures of this world, but don't neglect your inner well-being. Don't be seduced into believing that there's some direct connection between the material world and your own feelings of contentment. If well-being is what you want – and it's what we all want – paradoxically to achieve that you should try to focus on the well-being of others.'

Later that evening, we three corgis retired with the Queen and Philip to a private sitting room, where the royal couple were soon engrossed in books they had recently obtained from the City of Westminster's traveling library. Our bellies were full – in Winston's case, with a great many honey-and-mustard cocktail sausages. Coals glowed in the fireplace. A sense of peace pervaded the room. This was to become one of my favourite times in the circadian rhythm, with the activities of the day behind us and the Queen to ourselves.

Three baskets had been laid out to one side of the fireplace, two of them furnished with well-worn, tartan rugs, the third, newly installed for me. Following the example of the other corgis, I stepped into 'my' basket and lay down, trying to get comfortable. It was snug and protected, with just the right amount of cushioning. I could see both my fellow corgis and our human companions. The room was perfectly cosy. But something was lacking.

Getting out of my basket I made my way towards Winston's. Watching me, I could tell he knew what I hoped for. As he showed no objection, I climbed in and curled up next to him.

The Queen and Phillip exchanged glances as I felt the warmth of his body next to mine. *This* was what I needed. The comfort of corgi.

'Tell me, Winston, how did you get your name?' I asked, sleepily.

'Ah, dear boy, how we get our names.' He sighed. 'One single name can mean so many different things. There are outward meanings and inner, esoteric meanings …'

I thought he was going to leave me in a state of deep and continuing mystery but I really didn't mind because he'd called me 'dear boy', and I was warm with the glow of acceptance. But from the basket next door, Margaret said, 'We royal corgis are all named after national leaders. In Winston's case, it was his courageous defence of Queen and country that gave him his name.'

'Well,' he said pensively, 'that was part of it.'

'Do tell!' I urged him.

'We were with Her Majesty on a beach near Balmoral,' he told me, chest rising, 'minding our own business and enjoying the weather. Suddenly two Rottweilers appeared from nowhere and raced towards us. I bared my teeth and went on the attack.'

'Rottweilers?' I couldn't believe he'd take on two huge, powerful dogs with such fearsome reputations. 'Did you see them off?'

'Security stepped in,' he said. 'But I showed the Queen how far I'd go. I'd fight them on the beaches.'

In the basket next door, Margaret cleared her throat. 'There's that other story too,' she said.

'Another?' I wondered if Winston had also pursued German Shepherds in the fields? Or bared his fangs at Dobermanns in the streets?

Margaret was quick to disillusion me. 'He has a penchant for cigar stubs,' she said.

'A misunderstanding,' insisted Winston. 'I was trying to get to some pizza. One of the staff had dumped the contents of an ashtray on top of it.'

'Uh-huh.' Margaret sounded unconvinced.

'And you, Margaret?' I intervened, not wishing a pleasant moment to turn ugly. 'How did you come to be named?'

'For my constant vigilance in the service of the Queen,' she replied snippily.

'That's one way of putting it,' chortled Winston. 'The real story is that she attacked a famous trade union leader at a garden party.'

'Only a nip to the ankles.'

'There was a lot of blood.'

'Well, it was downright theft,' she snapped. 'He'd stuffed his overcoat pockets full of apple Danishes.'

There was a moment while I imagined the trade union leader, limping across the lawns of Buckingham Palace, his coat pockets filled with contraband pastries and socks drenched in blood. The Rottweilers halting in their tracks on the beach. Winston snuffling for pizza in the midst of burned-out cigars.

'I wonder what I'll end up being called,' I mused.

It was a while before Winston answered. 'These things aren't usually rushed.'

'Nor should they be,' chimed Margaret.

Winston exhaled sleepily, while I closed my eyes, snuggling up closer.

'Quite so,' said he.

Dozing in our baskets, I reflected on all that had happened during that eventful day. The meeting with Lord Cranleigh that morning and what the Queen had told him. The psychologist that evening, and how he'd made the same distinction between outer and inner.

The more I mulled it over, the more it occurred to me how both of them seemed to be saying the same thing. The Queen used plain words, but I recognised now that when she'd said we shouldn't confuse outward appearance with inner qualities because our well-being depended on it, she had been hinting at a much deeper truth. One with an importance going well beyond the floppy ear of a single corgi, but that most certainly included me too. Because it was thanks to the Queen's understanding about the true cause of happiness that she had dispatched Tara to my rescue when she'd heard what I faced at the hands of Mr Grimsley. Tara's neighbour's daughter, having just been to The Crown, had repeated to Tara over the fence what she'd just heard Mr Grimsley saying. Tara, in turn, had told Her Majesty. Acting on her concern for others – in this case me – the Queen had been engaged in the pursuit of *eudemonia*.

Glancing up from the book she was reading, for a moment her eyes met mine – and she smiled. Curled next to Winston, I wagged my stump. It didn't matter to the Queen that my ear was floppy, and so for the first time that I could ever remember, nor did it matter to me. Inner qualities, not outer appearances. If this was what well-being felt like, I pondered, I looked forward to enjoying more of it.

In the weeks that followed, I adjusted to my new life as a royal corgi. And my new homes. Palaces and castles with large rooms containing not a single corgi quickly began to seem the norm. I became familiar not only with the royal family, but with the household staff who attended them. It wasn't long before I had been the Queen's corgi for longer that I had been the Grimsleys', and my unfortunate start in life began to recede to nothing more than an unhappy memory. Which, I thought, was where the Grimsleys would remain.

But, my fellow subject, I was mistaken.

One morning we three corgis were in the lady-in-waiting's Buckingham Palace office, in a favourite sunspot on a sumptuous rug between the desks of Tara and Sophia. Tara was going through the day's mail when she snorted in a most unladylike way.

'Seriously?!' she exclaimed, pushing back her chair, unable to resist stepping over to share a particular letter with Sophia. All three of us looked up as Sophia quickly scanned the letter.

'Outrageous!' she agreed, her gypsy eyes flashing.

Both ladies looked directly at me.

The letter was from Mrs Patricia Gwendolyn Grimsley. She had been watching TV news, and the coverage of a charity function, when she noticed that one of 'her' corgis had joined the royal household. She and her husband, loyal Kennel Club members, were pleased to see their dearest, all-time favourite puppy had been acquired by Her Majesty. How, they wished to know, should they apply for a Royal Warrant, now that they were established as purveyors of corgis to the Queen's household?

'Never wanted to hear from me again!' Tara was indignant. 'The nerve of the woman!'

'Oh, you'll *have* to reply,' Sophia's eyes sparkled mischievously. 'Sign your letter "Lying Toerag, Her Majesty's lady-in-waiting".'

The two women burst out laughing.

'Didn't she make you promise never to say where you got him?' asked Tara.

'She did. Solemnly.' Tara returned to her desk. 'Which makes my decision easy.'

Leaning forward under her desk, she fed the letter into a shredder which whirred noisily.

'The only royal treatment she deserves is a one-way trip to the Tower of London.'

'The Queen can send people to the Tower?' I turned to the other corgis, instantly sensing a reputation as sinister as the shed.

'She can.' Margaret's eyes glowed with fervour.

'But doesn't,' confirmed Winston.

Well, I thought, that's what makes Her Majesty different from Mrs Grimsley.

It was not long after this that a very different item of correspondence arrived, one which Tara had no hesitation showing the Queen. It consisted of a single, but extraordinary photograph of an elephant silhouetted at sunset, and had been sent from Africa by Anthony Cranleigh, son of the lord. Along with the photograph was a short, handwritten note, which Tara read aloud as Her Majesty admired the photograph.

'Your Majesty, I am quite sure this will never reach you, but I just wanted to write it anyway to express my heartfelt thanks. All through my teenage years I wanted to be a wildlife photographer, but my father kept insisting this wasn't a 'proper' job, and that I should follow him into investment banking instead. Something you said to him recently made him change his mind. I don't know what it was, but it has allowed me to follow my dream, for which I am truly grateful. I would like you to have this photograph from my first visit to Kenya.'

'Very nice,' said the Queen, gazing at the photograph.

Winston and I exchanged a glance.

'So, *that* was what that whole thing was about? My floppy ear? Being guided by the right priorities?'

'Look sharp,' said he.

Two

I wish I could tell you that after my move from Slough to Windsor I lived happily ever after. If only I could report that my life was an endless succession of intriguing encounters by day and cosy fireside dozes with the royal family by night. That the inspiring presence of Her Majesty, the growing companionship of Winston and Margaret, and regular bouts of canapé-eating in gilded chambers all combined to a life of unalloyed bliss.

Alas, I cannot.

While it was a huge relief to have been rescued from the Grimsleys, and while the Queen and all those around her could not have been nicer, when I think back to those early days as a royal corgi, a shadow falls over me.

More than anything I am filled with shame.

There really isn't a nice way to say this, so I will just have to come out with it. I will risk the fact that, within the space of the next paragraph – or perhaps one or two after that – you are going to snap this book shut with a gasp of disappointment. Perhaps a furrow will wrinkle your brow as you wonder why you have wasted so much as a minute reading the work of a canine as deficient as me. But the facts must be faced. Steel yourself, my fellow subject, for the following painful

Truth is one that must be addressed: when I first joined the royal family, I was not palace-trained.

Instruction of that variety had been a haphazard affair at the Grimsleys'. With three litters of pups in one small home, accidents were frequent. We puppies were still emerging into the world, supervision was light, and in the chaos of the house, indiscretions were overlooked or even went unnoticed.

Not so at Buckingham Palace. Or any of the royal residences, come to that. I shudder to remember how, on my very first morning, I relieved myself, producing a rapidly growing puddle on the highly polished wooden floor directly outside the Queen's private rooms. On that occasion, within moments security had scooped me up and taken me to the small garden outside the staff scullery downstairs, where all such activity was to occur.

Several similar such incidents happened over the next few days, on each occasion, one of the staff whisking me outside. I cringe when I remember my behaviour. I suppose as a puppy I didn't yet have full control of my bodily functions. Nor was I at all clear about what part of the property was the den, and what part was not the den at Windsor Castle. Or Buckingham Palace. Or Balmoral. Or Sandringham. It was all so confusing!

The only consolation was that my various mishaps hadn't occur in the presence of anyone who mattered. By which, of course, I mean the Queen and her family. Or at least, they hadn't happened yet.

But then there came the time that Kate and a very young Prince George were making a visit to his great grandmamma at Windsor. The two were shown into a sitting room, to wait briefly while Her Majesty finished an official engagement, we three corgis offering an enthusiastic welcome, enjoying the lavish affection Kate bestowed on us.

Perhaps it was because I was the newest, and by far the smallest, addition to the household that Kate seemed especially indulgent of me, fondling my ears and rubbing my tummy with gusto. As all three of us corgis scampered about her and George, my excitement quite got the better of me. Suddenly I was peeing on the carpet.

'Oh dear, I think someone's having an accident!' laughed Kate.

A butler quickly seized me as Winston glanced askance and Margaret looked positively scandalised by my behaviour. Taken outside to the scullery garden, by the time I was returned to the room, a short while later, the Queen and Kate were sitting on a sofa, little George between them. Evidence of my incontinence formed a dark stain on the carpet, but if Her Majesty noticed, she made no mention of it. Nor did her attitude towards me seem to change in any way.

Had I got away with it?

It was during those earliest days at Windsor that I met one of the Queen's most intriguing advisers. His visit wasn't like the others in Her Majesty's official calendar, each of which would be confirmed weeks in advance and discussed at the start of each day with her private secretary, Julian. It happened on an overcast morning, when heavy mists veiled the river Thames and much of the castle was cloaked in gloom, one of those days in which the momentous events and historic figures of the past seemed invoked, unseen but living presences in this ancient royal castle.

We three corgis were snoozing at Tara's feet, after our morning walk, when Winston raised his head as though in response to a bell. Ears pricked up and head cocked to one side, he was tuning into some sound inaudible to me.

Turning to Margaret and me he said, 'Michael's here,' before jumping to his feet and making for the door. Because Margaret followed suit, so did I.

'Do they serve canapés when Michael visits?' I asked, wanting to demonstrate my evolving knowledge of how things worked around here.

'Of course not!' Margaret responded firmly, looking at me as if I was mad even to suggest it.

I realised that she was in one of her 'difficult' moods and hastened my pace to catching up with Winston.

'Who's Michael?' I asked.

'That, dear boy, is a question to which we'd all like to know the answer.'

'But you've met him before?'

'Many times.'

'Then you must have some idea?'

Winston snorted, realising that his enigmatic answers were wasted on a pup.

'You were at this morning's diary meeting?'

'Yes.'

'Did Julian mention a visit from Michael?'

'No.'

'Does the Queen ever receive unscheduled visitors?'

'Um ...' I thought I knew the correct answer, but was feeling less than confident after Margaret's fierce response to my question about canapés.

'Never!' Winston provided the answer with a decided 'ah' about the second syllable of that word. 'She does not. She is the Queen. Nobody just drops in to see Her Majesty. Nobody, that is, except Michael.'

'And you're sure he's here?' I was following Winston down a long corridor.

'Quite sure.'

'But, I mean, how do you know?'

'I'm tuned in,' said Winston. 'Just as I expect you will become too, dear boy.' He seemed to have made some judgement about me and was paying me a compliment.

I wagged my stump.

'We dogs hear sound frequencies that humans cannot.'

'Really?' This was news to me. 'Like magic?'

'Not magic,' said Winston. 'It comes from within.'

He shot a glance over his shoulder towards Margaret, and I realised that he was drawing me into his confidence. 'It evolves quite naturally over time. Of course some of us are more receptive than others. We need to be open to it.'

Margaret, I gathered, was not open.

We emerged in a hallway at the bottom of the stairs that led up to the Queen's private apartment, the very same stairs Tara had ascended when she'd first brought me to Windsor Castle. The figure in the hallway had his back to us when we arrived, but hearing the sound of our paws on the carpet, he turned.

'Ah, the welcoming committee!'

He was a substantial man, tall and broad shouldered, but the most immediate thing I noticed about him was the lightness he conveyed. Perhaps it was the enlivening quality of his very clear, blue eyes. Perhaps the inviting warmth about his features. As Winston scampered briskly towards him, Margaret bypassed him, seeming more interested in a newly installed pedestal table.

'And *you've* joined them!' It was as if he recognised me from somewhere before. 'What fun we're all going to have!'

As he bent to pat Winston and me, I nuzzled his hand, taking in the scent of him. It was a herbaceous and strangely compelling aroma that seemed to connect him to an ancient, more pastoral time. His appearance was that of a mature man, his hair snowy and face lined, but as I looked directly into his eyes for the first time, I felt drawn to a state of timelessness. Along with the lightness was a feeling of ineffable peace. Even in those first few moments, I realised that Michael was unlike anyone I'd ever encountered.

He began making his way up the stairs to Her Majesty's apartment. Pausing on the landing, he regarded the soldier in chain mail with solemnity, the two acknowledging each other with respectful inclines of their heads, before Michael continued upwards. We entered the private apartment and made our way to the door leading to the Queen's office.

Michael hadn't so much as knocked on the door when we heard Her Majesty's voice, 'Michael – is that you?'

'Indeed, your Majesty.'

'Do come.'

As he stepped into her office, the Queen rose from her desk. Her visitor bowed.

'Your timing is, as always, impeccable,' she said.

When other people had come to her office, she would show them to one of the armchairs, before sitting on another. But she made no attempt to suggest where Michael should sit, and instead returned to her the chair at her desk, watching as he stood at the window looking out at the swirling grey mist, his back towards her.

'Difficult week?' There was understanding gentleness in his rich, bass voice as he looked out over the shrouded landscape.

'Like wading through treacle,' said Her Majesty. 'Sometimes one can't help questioning why one's doing this.'

'Mmm.'

'Would people, in fact, prefer it if we weren't here?'

At the window, her visitor nodded slowly.

'It's about relevance, Michael.' I had never heard the Queen express her doubts so freely. In fact, had I not been sitting at her feet, I wouldn't have believed anyone who told me she could even entertain such dark thoughts.

'One sometimes feels like such an anachronism,' she continued. 'From a rational point of view, there is no place for a monarchy at all.' She sighed. 'It is utterly undemocratic. There is no logic to it. And yet ...'

After a pause he turned from the window to face her, his blue eyes seeming almost luminescent in the darkness of the room. 'And yet,' he repeated, 'reason gets us only so far. Few of our life's most important decisions, and none of mankind's grandest undertakings, are driven by reason alone. The greatest works of art, the most important scientific endeavours, the building of empires, the pursuit of love, dreams and passions – none of our most significant endeavours are propelled by mere logic.

'You, my Queen, are so much more than what you can or cannot do. Your mere presence is one of the most universal and powerful symbols of mankind.'

Just as I had never heard Her Majesty voice her reservations, nor had I ever heard someone speak to the Queen with such sweeping authority. There was respect in his voice, to be sure, but a guiding purpose that seemed almost fatherly.

'You are the embodiment of continuity and the well-being of your people. You represent stability and hope. Whatever your own personal reservations, as sovereign you are a beacon for the forces of light in a degenerate age.

'This land, and the culture that springs from it, has been a cradle of ancient spirituality since time immemorial. For thousands of years our people strove to live in harmony with the spirit they found in everything. God was present in nature and they sought Him in holy – healing – places. In caves, and springs, and mountains, in rituals and pilgrimages through which they placed themselves in resonance with those who'd been before.

'Most Christian experience has been of this same, intuitive nature. The mass chanted in a language only the priests knew, the soaring spires, the stained glass and the incense – what was all this if not an invocation to experience a more transcendent state of consciousness? Divine presence?

'In only a few hundred years, most of it has been lost. The current obsession with the material world, with consumerism, can make one feel that somehow our people have taken the wrong turning.'

'Haven't they?' interjected the Queen, her voice cool as stone in that grey morning.

'Complete immersion can be useful to discover something's limitations,' Michael said wryly. 'And we are already witnessing the return of the pendulum to a greener and more balanced way of being. Spirit is being rediscovered.' His voice was tremulous with feeling. 'No longer called "spirit", but "energy". Einstein and the quantum scientists have shown that matter and energy co-exist. That energy is in everything. Our true purpose in life –' he paused '– is to awaken to our own energy, and to use it for the well-being of all.'

In the stillness we considered the importance of what he had just said, before he told Her Majesty, 'You already know this, of course. Your special role is to inspire it in others. Which you do so well, holding up a mirror to them, inviting them to see how they match up to their own purest nature.'

The Queen reflected on this in silence.

'You play the most vital part in an esoteric lineage reaching back for a millennia. Like your ancestors, you do so through symbols and ritual. Is it a coincidence that the language and culture of this small island has such sweeping influence on the rest of the world?

There was a lengthy pause before Her Majesty finally spoke, somewhat wryly. 'Thank you, Michael, for reminding me of my most awesome responsibilities.'

It was at this precise moment, a time when I was listening to the most profound words I'd ever heard spoken, that I felt a sudden and unaccountable urge. Getting up from under the Queen's desk, I walked some distance towards a bookshelf, where I squatted and began to relieve myself.

And it wasn't just a puddle.

As it happened, both Winston and Margaret were dozing next to the Queen's desk. But Her Majesty and Michael both looked at me.

'Oh, dear,' said the Queen.

Michael chuckled. 'A reminder to keep our feet on the ground.'

'Hmm. He's still very little and in training,' said Her Majesty. 'There's no point trying to stop them mid-way through …' She was far too polite to refer directly to what I was doing.

'Quite so, Your Majesty,' agreed Michael. Before adding, after a pause, 'He has yet to become an alchemist.'

The Queen looked puzzled. 'A corgi? Turning base metal into gold?'

'A metaphor for personal transformation. The true purpose of alchemy is about reining in our baser instincts –' he nodded towards me '– and realizing our highest potential.'

'I never thought alchemy had anything to do with me. Or corgis,' she replied. 'It seems I was mistaken.'

Michael nodded. 'It's another universal archetype. The idea actually comes from an ancient Egyptian word for the black earth of the Nile. It was only from such darkness that life, in all its richness, could spring forth. In the East there is a similar concept – no mud, no lotus. Only through suffering is transcendence possible.'

'So we should all strive to be alchemists?' confirmed the Queen.

'Indeed.' Outside, great banks of grey clouds suddenly lifted, and for the first time that morning, a shaft of sunlight broke through. 'We can give purpose to our dissatisfaction when we find a way to use it, when it gives rise to a flowering of exquisite beauty.'

They seemed to have come the full circle, back to Her Majesty's feelings when Michael had first stepped into the room, except that now there were the stirrings of new possibilities.

'Thank you, Michael, for your inspiration.' The Queen smiled, rising from her chair. 'You bring fresh hope.'

Opposite, Michael brought his palms to his heart and bowed briefly.

They turned to where I crouched, ashamed, beside my deposit.

'I'd better summon help,' said Her Majesty.

'Quite so.'

As they walked to the door, I joined the two other corgis following them. Winston shot me a consoling glance which made me feel only worse. Margaret ignored me completely.

'Just one thing.' The Queen paused for a moment in the reception room outside her office. 'The transcendence you speak of, that's public service, is it not?'

'It may well take that form, Your Majesty. And you use your position to give comfort and inspiration to many. But it doesn't have to be about the grand gesture or the trappings of state. It is my deep conviction –' Michael seemed to be communicating with more than words alone '– that doing small acts with great love is our most precious gift, and not only for those we are helping. It is a wonderful paradox that when we help others, we, ourselves, are the first to benefit.'

A short while later Michael left and the Queen summoned a footman to remove all evidence of my wretched lack of toilet-training. We followed her to the office of her lady-in-waiting while this was happening.

If you are concerned, my fellow subject, that this chapter will provide an exhaustive listing of my every bowel movement as a puppy, allow me to put your mind at rest. In the weeks that followed our meeting with Michael, I continued to have accidents, oversights and mishaps. Eventually, however, I got the hang of it through a combination of self-control as well as learning what was, and was not, our den. Looking back you might even say that the meeting with Michael was the lowest point in my palace-training were it not for the fact that it was only through my lack of self-control that we discovered the true meaning of the word alchemy. And how it signified one's life's purpose.

For my own part, I needed to control my impulses. To learn that there was a time and place, which did not include the polished, wooden hallway flooring or ancient Persian carpets that bedecked the various royal residences.

As for the Queen, her life was already the embodiment of so much of what Michael had said: the power of symbols; deeds, not words; transcendence through service to others. But I detected something new in the weeks that followed. Something that hearkened back to his wisdom about doing small acts with great love.

For several weeks each summer while the royal family was elsewhere, parts of Buckingham Palace were opened to the public. Every day from late August through September, long queues would form from early in the morning as people from all over the world eagerly awaited their chance to visit the most famous royal residence in the world. The tourists included groups of all kinds – the elderly, schools, and a wide range of nationalities – whose passage through the palace was managed by a security and visitor team with well-practiced efficiency.

As it happened, on one such day the Queen had to cut short her stay at Sandringham to meet the Commonwealth secretary general in London, where she would sign into effect a new trade agreement. The meeting, to be held at

Buckingham Palace, was not expected to take more than twenty minutes, after which the Queen would travel on to Windsor.

Arrangements for the brief visit to Buckingham Palace by Her Majesty and the secretary general caused the Queen's head of security, Huchens, no end of concern. A large, muscular Highlander in his early forties, he was a former senior figure in the SAS and had received several decorations for gallantry from the Queen herself. Margaret had told me approvingly how he possessed what she termed 'gunfighter nerves', and had no startle reflex at all. The loudest explosion could happen right beside him, or he could be on the receiving end of the most dire threat, and his expression would be completely unaltered. Only the best of the best could be entrusted to take care of Her Majesty's security.

Allowing large numbers of unknown people close proximity to the monarch always presented a danger. The age-old protocol of flying the royal standard over the palace when Her Majesty was in residence was quickly dismissed. Working out how to get the Queen and her VIP visitor in and out of the building on a day when it was open to the public presented a logistical challenge which the burly Scot pondered from every angle.

On the day in question, Her Majesty, accompanied by all three royal corgis, was whisked into the palace and upstairs to the stateroom where she was to meet the secretary general. While waiting, she made her way to a glass door which overlooked the line of people about to be admitted to the palace. From behind a sheer curtain she watched, in particular, as a group of a dozen or so teenage schoolboys in the blazers of St George's Boys School, restlessly pushed and shoved each other, despite the futile protests of their female teacher. Beside the Queen, we three corgis watched as a particularly large boy jumped on the shoes of another one, a pale, bespectacled and much slighter fellow. Even from the upstairs window the pain being inflicting by the brute was quite evident.

Her Majesty shuddered.

There was little time to contemplate the horrors of schoolboy bullying, however, because within minutes the Queen's guest was being announced. He and a small entourage swept into the room for a most cordial meeting during which Her Majesty signed the new trade treaty into effect. It was one, declared the secretary general, which would improve the economic prospects of literally millions of people. By abandoning trade tariffs and taxes, many more businesses would be encouraged to increase their trade, as well as the number of people they employed, leading to better conditions for many.

Within half an hour, the secretary general was leaving and the Queen was standing by for a signal from Huchens, who was with her in the room, to advise that the coast was clear to return downstairs to her waiting car. Standing, handbag over her arm, Her Majesty looked out the one-way glass of an internal door, facing down a staircase to the hallway below, through which a steady stream of visitors passed. A decorative red rope looped across the bottom of the stairs, with a 'Private. No Entry' sign.

As it happened, the same unruly gang of schoolboys we had previously watched outside were now passing through the hall, and had somehow become separated from their teacher. This time, the fruity tones of the bully rose up the stairs. 'Simpson, you wuss!' He cracked the boy over the head. 'Seeing you know all the kings and queens of England, go up there and have tea with Queenie.'

'Dare ya!' A colleague challenged him.

'Yeah – you great girl's blouse!' Another kid jabbed him in the ribs.

'Double dare ya!' challenged the bully again, knocking him in the back of the leg so he almost collapsed.

'See if the Queen of England gives a shit about ya!'

Moments later, pale and frightened, the dishevelled Simpson was stepping across the red rope and fleeing up the stairs. Evidently prepared to do almost anything to get away from his tormentors, as soon as he was out of sight of the group, he stood behind a pillar, panting heavily.

The purpose of the red rope at the foot of the stairs was in fact purely ceremonial, all of the doors at the top of the stairs being securely locked. Not that Simpson knew this as he stood, crumpled and harassed, waiting for his colleagues to go further through the hallway.

Only a short distance away, on the other side of a glass door veiled with curtains, the Queen had been closely following everything that happened.

'Huchens,' she asked, as they continued to stand, waiting, 'will you bring that boy to me?'

Her Majesty's head of security said nothing, but wore a somewhat quizzical expression as he unlocked a side door and made his way outside.

The schoolboy was aghast to be confronted by Huchens who looked, all six feet four of him, every inch the SAS warrior. 'I didn't mean to trespass, sir!' he spluttered.

'This way, young man.' Huchens guided him by the arm along the landing. 'There's someone who wishes to speak to you.'

When Simpson was ushered into the room and found himself only a few feet from the Queen, his shaken expression became more complicated, a mix of surreality and extreme nervousness.

'How do you do?' said Her Majesty.

With the utmost formality, Simpson folded his right arm over his waist and bent to almost a right angle.

'Good morning, Miss,' he said, when once again upright. Before correcting himself. 'I mean, ma'am.' Then unnecessarily correcting himself again. 'Your Royal Highness.'

'Majesty,' Huchens directed him in a stage whisper.

'Your Royal Majesty.' The boy was tying himself in knots.

'Just "Your Majesty",' corrected Huchens.

The Queen glanced at Huchens with an expression of droll censure.

'What is your name, young man?' she asked.

'Andrew Simpson.'

'And tell me, are the other boys always so ... beastly to you?'

He seemed greatly relieved to discover that the Queen was on his side. 'Some of them didn't want to come 'cos it's school holidays. But I won the group visit for the school as a prize.'

'Really? For what?'

'Being able to recite all the kings and queens of England since 1066, Miss ... erm ... Your Majesty.'

'That's quite an achievement.' There was genuine approval in the Queen's voice. 'I wonder how you manage.'

'I place each name in a different room of an imaginary palace. Memory technique.'

'And what made you wish to learn them?'

'I want to study at Oxford.' In the pause that followed the boy's face clouded. 'But ...'

Her Majesty stepped closer, fiddling for a moment with the strap of her handbag. 'Go on,' she urged him with a nod.

'Jenkins and the others –' He gestured.

'The bully?' confirmed the Queen.

'Yes. He says he's going to make my life a living hell next term, Your Majesty. He says he's going to play the bagpipes every single study break so I fail the entrance exams. I wouldn't put it past him.' Simpson seemed to have got over the shock of finding himself in the presence of the Queen and was talking more freely. 'Bannerman had a nervous breakdown when Jenkins had it in for him. He had to leave school. And Weaver is still on antidepressants. You should see Jenkins turn the fire hose on the freshers when they're in the changing rooms!'

'What does your headmaster say about all this?'

'Miss Thwaites.' The boy looked even more forlorn as he tilted his head downstairs. 'Every time she tries discipline, Jenkins's father goes ballistic. He's a rich businessman and is on the school board.'

'I see,' said Her Majesty.

He was a pitiful sight, Andrew Simpson, intimidated by the prospect of months of bullying ending in academic failure. Approaching him, I sniffed his ankles and wagged my stump in a consolatory way.

'Bagpipes?' queried the Queen. 'Most unusual.'

'He's the leader of the school band. He's very loud.'

'Hmm.' Her Majesty stepped even closer and looked her unexpected guest in the eye. 'You know what bullies want to do, Andrew, don't you? They want to destroy your self-confidence. To make you believe that you can't do something. To give up hope.'

Following her intently, the boy nodded.

'Well, let me tell you something.' Her tone changed to one of defiance. 'I don't personally know anyone who can recite the complete list of kings and queens of England since 1066.'

The boy's Adam's apple bobbed as he swallowed.

'It's a very impressive achievement, and there's no reason why you shouldn't go on to greater things. You may have an *annus horribilis* ahead of you. But you will get through it. A few years from now, Jenkins will be nothing but a memory, but you will have a degree from Oxford. How would that make you feel?'

'Pretty amazing.' Her Majesty's uninvited guest pushed his spectacles up his nose as he drew himself up.

The Queen's words, combined with the fact that he was being personally advised by the monarch in Buckingham Palace, seemed to be filling him with new purpose.

'You must never forget that you are a very special person.' In an act of unusual friendliness, the Queen placed her gloved hand on the boy's arm.

His eyes were gleaming.

'In all the years Buckingham Palace has been open to the public, I have never received a visitor until today. Isn't that right, Huchens.' She glanced over.

'Correct, Your Majesty.'

'Don't forget that, Andrew Simpson.' She smiled as his lips trembled, and he blinked back tears.

Huchens' phone bleeped and the head of security gestured to the Queen that all was ready for her departure.

Realising that his audience was over, Andrew grasped at his blazer pocket in some frustration. 'I wish I'd brought some paper, I'd really like to ask for your autograph,' he said.

'Write to me care of Huchens,' replied the Queen, extending her hand to shake his. Then somewhat mysteriously, 'I'm sure our paths will cross again.'

Some minutes later, we three corgis were sharing the back of a Range Rover, driven by Bradshaw, the Queen's regular London driver. Huchens occupied the front passenger seat. The plan was for us to make our way out of a side entrance, where unmarked police cars idled in waiting. As we were proceeding slowly in that direction, however, something caught Her Majesty's attention: the group of St George's boys were walking towards the front gates.

'Bradshaw!' commanded the Queen. 'Over to those schoolboys. I'd like a word.'

Huchens raised his eyebrows. 'We must exit through the side gates,' he confirmed with Bradshaw.

'Yes, yes,' said Her Majesty, 'but a minute's delay is of no consequence.'

The boys had to clear the driveway to make way for the Range Rover. Which drew to a halt in their midst. As the tinted glass of the rear window lowered to reveal Her Majesty, the effect on the group could not have been more instant or dramatic. I know – I was sitting on the back seat right beside her and watched as every last one of them regarded her with an expression of stunned incredulity.

'I've just had a nice meeting with your prize winner, Andrew.' The Queen nodded towards where he was standing. 'He tells me there are some boys at the school who wish to disrupt his studies.' Her gaze moved from one end of the group to the other, before pausing on the class brute who was standing, shirt untucked from his trousers, the knot of his tie tugged halfway down his chest. 'Jenkins?'

The boy opened his mouth several times, but no words came out of it, before he finally managed in a hoarse tone, 'Yes, your um … Queen Elizabeth.'

'I want you to make sure no harm comes to him.'

Jenkins had turned remarkably pale.

'Can I rely on you?'

'Yes.'

She studied him with an inscrutable expression for quite a while before saying, 'Andrew tells me you're rather good on the bagpipes. If you behave yourself we might arrange to have your band to the Braemar Gathering.'

Jenkins glanced at Simpson somewhat nervously. 'That would be … very nice.'

'No doubt Andrew will report back to me next time I see him.' Her Majesty turned and nodded once to the headmistress. 'Miss Thwaites.'

'Your Majesty.' The headmistress was clearly startled to be addressed directly by the Queen, taking several seconds to recover her composure before performing a somewhat stilted curtsey.

'Oh, and Jenkins. I think you'll find I'm the Queen of the United Kingdom, not the Queen of England. And I do actually give a … whatever it was you mentioned.'

Pressing a button, the tinted window rolled back up and she disappeared from their view.

'Drive on, Bradshaw.'

Huchens waited for Bradshaw to clear the palace, accompanied by the usual police escort, before he turned to the Queen. 'That was very nicely done, ma'am, if I may say so.'

'You may.'

'I don't think the boy will have any more trouble.'

'Let's hope not,' said Her Majesty. 'You know, Huchens, I came here today to sign into effect measures that will bring economic relief to millions of people. But what just happened was curiously rewarding.'

'For everyone involved.'

'Small acts with great love.'

'Quite right too,' he agreed, with a very Scottish roll of the 'r'.

That evening, having travelled to Windsor, the Queen was joined by Charles for private dinner. Having not seen each other in person for several weeks, and Charles being no fan of lengthy telephone conversations, there was much to catch up on.

'Did you enjoy Sandringham?' he asked, knowing how much his mother usually enjoyed her time there.

'Very much. I spent quite some time at the stables. It's wonderful to see the new bloodlines coming through.'

The two of them were sitting in the dining room of her apartment, a butler in attendance and we three corgis lying at their feet. Charles had been known, in the past, to slip the occasional unwanted morsel of food under the table, and Winston had positioned himself for exactly such an eventuality.

'Were the horses pleased to see you?' asked Charles, a hint of mischief in his tone.

'So Cameron told me.' This was evidently something of a running joke.

'Frisky?' confirmed Charles.

'That's the effect he claims I have on them just by being at Sandringham.' Her Majesty sounded doubtful.

'You know, I've been reading a book that makes me wonder if there might be something in what Cameron's always said. It seems that animals are much more aware of things than we generally give them credit for.'

I cocked my head at her. Winston tilted his own grizzled features in a knowing fashion. Margaret showed little interest in the conversation.

'There's some pretty convincing evidence about things like dogs knowing when their owners are coming home.'

'Really?' said the Queen.

'They did this study setting up video recorders in people's houses. It would show the family pooch getting up and going to the front doormat within minutes of his owner leaving work to come home. The owners varied their routine and changed their leaving times and so on. The uncanny thing is how consistent it was, not just for one or two dogs, but for a whole lot of different pets. They seemed to have this way of knowing. It doesn't seem too far a stretch to suggest that maybe the horses can sense certain things too.'

Looking Winston in the eye, I remembered back to the morning that Michael had visited. How the Queen's oldest and wisest corgi had suddenly looked up from where we'd been resting in the office of the ladies-in-waiting and made his way downstairs. There had been no need for bells or whistles. Winston had simply known. And, sure enough, as soon as we found our way downstairs, we had found Michael.

'When you ride a horse over time,' observed Her Majesty, an experienced rider, 'you can develop a very definite sense of connection. Especially when you and the horse do a lot of things together – jumping and so on. It goes beyond the mechanical, the physical.'

'The jockeys often say they communicate by visualising a particular result.'

'Yes.'

'And what's that if it isn't some form of telepathy?' asked Charles.

The Queen digested this observation in silence, before she murmured, 'Whatever you do, don't share your thoughts with anyone who might …'

Charles groaned. 'I know. The whole thing would be turned into a circus. The media would have me holding seances with the corgis in between chattering away to my plants.'

'Exactly. Better to keep one's mouth shut and provide a silent symbol of continuity.'

'Very wise,' said Charles.

'I was reminded of just that by Michael only recently.'

'Ah, Michael.' Charles's tone was wistful. 'When *am* I going to meet him?'

'You will,' said the Queen.

'You've been saying that for nearly thirty years.'

I looked at Winston in astonishment. Michael was not only a regular visitor to the Queen, but he enjoyed a position of rare privilege and trust. So why hadn't he met Charles? Did this mean that the royal corgis were better acquainted with one of Her Majesty's closest advisers than the heir to the throne?

'I've been saying it,' the Queen said simply, 'because it's true.'

Winston returned my look with an expression of amusement and very deep enigma. Like Charles, I wondered if royal life was always so very mysterious. And why Winston had missed the morsel of lamb which Charles had generously slipped onto the dining room carpet.

Three

There is, in Buckingham Palace, a wardrobe which only a handful of people know about. Its very existence is one of the Queen's most closely guarded secrets. Its purpose would shock even her closest aides, and it is the source of her security team's worst headaches. Not that there's anything especially unusual about either the wardrobe or its contents. It's the use to which those contents are put that few people would believe.

I discovered this unseen dimension of Her Majesty's activities within a few months of joining the royal family. Winston and Margaret had been left at Windsor that particular week, having come down with a tummy bug for which they were both being treated. Which was why I was the Queen's only metropolitan corgi – and how I was to become the unwitting cause of one of the worst security breaches in recent decades.

It began on a beautiful April morning. The Queen rose earlier than usual, and spent some time looking down the Mall towards Trafalgar Square, taking in the verdant greenness of St James's Park, the flower beds adazzle with the yellow freshness of daffodils. A light breeze rippled through the open window, bringing with it the stirrings of spring.

There is a particular quality about Buckingham Palace, especially those front rooms which face directly onto the

Mall. While Windsor Castle, steeped in royal history, lends itself to withdrawal, reflection and mystic communion with the spirits of kings and queens down the ages, Buckingham Palace is the royal family's shop-front. The epicentre of a throbbing metropolis, it is the heart not only of one nation, but of a global Commonwealth. When gazing down the Mall, it is as though you are directly facing into the main artery of the world. And when it is Her Majesty who is standing there, it is as if she gives new life to a flow of energy, a charge that sparks down invisible pathways as powerful as they are ancient, leaping across synapses, channelling through countries and continents, strengthening ties and renewing connections, returning back as an impulse of gathering vibrancy and force.

For the longest time she stood at the windows, looking out. Then she made a decision. Instead of breakfast, she summoned Huchens.

'I'd like to make an excursion.'

'Very good. I'll see to the arrangements.'

Huchens had answered with his usual Scottish burr, but, as I watched, I noticed his face blush a shade pinker. What was it about an excursion that perturbed him?

'When would Your Majesty like to go?'

'Now.'

'I see.'

I whimpered softly, and the Queen looked at me. I could tell that something was up. An 'excursion' – whatever it meant exactly – sounded like something I would like very much to be a part of. The same idea evidently occurred to Her Majesty.

'Huchens, would the security dogs be available?'

I had met these great, prowling beasts. Two German shepherds and a Dobermann with whom I, and the other corgis, maintained a wary upstairs-downstairs relationship.

Huchens glanced in my direction. 'I can see where you're going with this, ma'am. I'll make enquiries.'

Her Majesty nodded. 'The Bow Room in fifteen minutes?'

'Very good, Your Majesty.'

Moments later I followed the Queen to her dressing room. And to the wardrobe that was kept permanently locked – except, I was discovering, for when Her Majesty went on an 'excursion'. Curious to know what she needed to retrieve, given that she was already dressed, I watched her find the key to the wardrobe from a hidey-hole in a drawer, undo the lock and – was it age that made her hand tremor slightly, or excitement? – reach inside.

As a corgi, I am no expert on the clothing worn by humans. As a male dog, barely out of puppyhood, I was perhaps even less sensitive to such matters. Nevertheless, even I was astonished by the transformation I witnessed. Her Majesty was changing into a pair of faded, blue Levis and a plastic anorak, before slipping into a pair of robust Nike trainers. This, even I could tell, was no apparel for a Queen. Not even Mrs Grimsley would have been seen in such attire.

Next, to my astonishment, Her Majesty retrieved something dark and hairy from the wardrobe and tugged it over her head – a wig! Followed, a short while later, by a cap with the intertwined initials NY emblazoned prominently on the front. Finally came the large and obviously fake Dolce & Gabbana sunglasses.

The transformation was complete!

As she donned her disguise, I noticed the Queen's posture changing. Her usual regal reserve was replaced by a casual jauntiness. Like a shape-shifter, she seemed to be morphing into a different kind of being.

'Come on, little one!' She leaned down, hands on her knees, with a playful expression. 'Walkies!'

It started well. Better than well. Being outside on a glorious day, free of the constraints of being inside with all the usual protocols, for a while we could all simply enjoy being alive on a spring morning. A number of secret service men had already been deployed by the time we left the security of the palace. I was some way ahead of the Queen, my own identity, if not disguised, then at least distracted from by the presence of the two German Shepherds with whom I trotted polite-ly, our leashes in the hands of a plainclothes police woman, Detective Lewis.

As it happened, the dog handler wasn't around at that hour of the morning, but because the purpose of the German shepherds was unofficial, that absence wasn't thought to mat-ter. Detective Lewis, it was believed, could easily handle a walk in the park.

Some distance behind us Her Majesty was accompanied by Huchens. There were more plainclothes policemen be-hind them. As we made our way through the leafy luxuriance of Buckingham Palace Gardens, I took in the beautiful shrubs and trees, so many different shades of green. The ornamental lakes, their fountains gushing plumes of silver in the morning light. There were some people about but we seemed to be shar-ing the gardens mainly with teeming birdlife. This included sev-eral flocks of ducks – a kind of bird I had never seen before. As they swam about the ponds, I watched them, fascinated. As they dived below the surface, only their bobbing tail feathers protruding, I became even more intrigued.

We had completed a wide circuit of the gardens and were on our way home when the temptation simply became too great. Twelve ducks stood in the middle of the lawn, a fair distance from the ponds. From some part of my being I hadn't even known existed up till then, I felt a sudden, urgent instinct … to herd them. Should they not be in the pond, rather than on the grass? The way they were waddling around and preening themselves seemed deliberately provocative. Impertinent! As a herding dog was it not my civic duty to tidy the place up?

Not to mention that it would be enormous fun.

I gave a jolt. As it happened, a split second before I did, Detective Lewis's phone vibrated in her pocket. In that vital moment she was caught off guard. To my own very great surprise – and joy – I was free!

Tugging the leash from her hand, I raced across the lawns. And was rewarded almost instantly with a loud squawking of alarm. Some of the ducks quacked into immediate take-off, shedding feathers as they went. Others were lurching frantically towards the pond as fast as their orange galoshes would take them. Barking with excitement, I raced in a wide arc, rounding them up like a seasoned pro.

I was thrilled. Energised. Empowered. Within seconds there wasn't a single duck remaining on the grass.

There were, however, quite a number of passers-by who had turned to watch my vigorous performance. Workers crossing the gardens on their way to work stared in my direction. Several early morning tourists paused and pointed. The word 'corgi!' came on the breeze. Then, in the next breath, 'Queen!'

For the first time I began to realise what I'd done.

Several men materialised from the atmosphere. I recognised them immediately as special branch detectives from the palace. They were approaching rapidly from either side while Detective Lewis and the two German shepherds hurried towards me.

I looked about to see that Huchens had changed direction. His SAS training no doubt kicking into action, he was leading Her Majesty from the scene of my hot pursuit, well away from where she might be noticed by association. Rather than returning to the palace through the gardens, he was leading her instead towards a pavement.

Within moments I was apprehended, my leash held much shorter and with noticeable firmness. Detective Lewis was evidently in no mood to play. In fact, any sense of spring-like zest had evaporated.

Even though the morning was just as clear and wonderful as it had been before my sortie, things seemed to have somehow shifted into a minor key. The rays of the sun felt cooler. The wind more bracing. Tension emanated down the leash from the police detective. The German shepherds were unsettled – I could see it in their disdainful, but somewhat envious, expressions.

The plainclothes special branch officers seemed to vanish as mysteriously as they had appeared. Detective Lewis was leading us in the direction of the pavement some distance behind Her Majesty.

There were few people on the pavement so early in the morning, and those who were took absolutely no notice of the Queen. Walking, hunched-up, over their phones, or caught up in whatever was playing through their earbuds, they walked right past her in a state of total self-absorption. Her Majesty gestured that Huchens should step ahead of her instead of blocking the whole pavement. And so we continued down a short distance of pavement on our return to the palace, outside the garden walls.

There was one, small intersection we needed to cross, and as we approached it, the traffic lights were red. Rather than expose the Queen by letting her stand on the corner, Huchens slowed his pace right down. There was only one shop on that particular stretch of the street. Palace Newsagency was a tiny store, barely larger than the Grimsleys' shed, with a door to one side and a hatch that opened directly onto the pavement, framed by that day's newspapers, neatly tucked into racks. There were also many glossy magazines, their headlines prominently displayed.

One of these caught Her Majesty's eye as she walked by at the greatly reduced speed set by Huchens. 'Equestrian world shocked …', began the headline of *Racing News*. The Queen halted, angling her head slightly in an attempt to read the first paragraph.

What, precisely, was the cause of the upset, she no doubt wondered? She paused only for a few moments. Seconds, perhaps.

But in that time an Indian man appeared from the shop. Wearing a flowing white shirt, his head completely bald, there was a radiance about his features. Touching his forehead, throat and heart with his folded hands in rapid succession while bowing, he said, 'Would you be liking this magazine, Your Majesty Elizabeth?'

By this stage, Detective Lewis and we dogs were only a few steps behind her.

'Oh, erm ....' I only rarely heard her Majesty hesitate. 'I think there's been a mistake,' she said, in her unmistakeable voice.

'Please.' He was already taking the paper from the rack and handing it to her. 'With a thousand blessings.'

'Well, thank you!' She accepted it, before Huchens had stepped back to guide her away firmly by the elbow.

He was leading her across at the green light when one of the plainclothes detectives slipped into the shop.

'That, um, wasn't supposed to happen,' he said.

'Not to be worrying,' replied the shop owner. 'Her Majesty Elizabeth is interested in the horses.'

The detective nodded briskly. 'I mean her unscheduled visit.'

'Oh.' The other shrugged, as if nothing out of the ordinary had happened. 'I know she likes to walk in the gardens.'

Perceiving a sudden, much graver security risk, the detective frowned. 'You do? How do you know?'

'I can tell she is walking close by sometimes.' The man smiled enigmatically. 'I can sense it here.' He touched his heart.

'Well.' The detective coughed. 'That's not my remit. But regarding today's ... visit –'

'Don't you be worrying.' The other reached out and touched him confidentially on the arm. 'My lips are completely sealed.'

After we returned to the palace, Her Majesty and I went upstairs, where she changed into more Queenly attire. Huchens hadn't said a word about the duck-chasing incident as we entered, but it was evidently on the Queen's mind as she emerged from her dressing chamber looking her usual, regal self.

'I hope you enjoyed your little romp this morning, young man.' She bent to pat me. I looked up at her adoringly, wagging my stump. 'Huchens wouldn't have enjoyed it at all. I fear we haven't heard the last of it.'

She was quite right, my fellow subject. We had not.

The two of us went downstairs for our respective breakfasts. It wasn't long after we had finished, and I was resting at Her Majesty's feet, that Huchens arrived in her sitting room.

'About this morning's security breach, ma'am,' he began, rolling his 'r's' severely. 'I wish to undertake a full, root and branch review.'

He went on to detail how Her Majesty's safety had been gravely compromised as a result of being accompanied by an untrained and ill-disciplined puppy. How the police detective's handling of me had been a serious and avoidable error. How the Queen's disguise had – as he had so often cautioned in the past – proven to be utterly unconvincing. Even the newsagent's comment about being able to 'sense' when the Queen was walking was reported with grim concern.

Looking up from her morning newspaper, Her Majesty took it all in her stride. 'Well, Huchens, I know it's your job to worry about these things but there's no need to overreact. You neglected to mention the main fault, which was that I stopped to read a headline.' She nodded towards where the magazine was lying on a nearby table.

'That was ...' Huchens searched for the right word '... regrettable.'

'What of it?' the Queen said with a shrug. 'The puppy couldn't resist the ducks. I couldn't resist the headline. We discovered our local newsagent to be psychic. No harm done.'

'But ma'am –'

'It's a nice morning. I enjoyed the air and the exercise.'

Huchens glanced out the window, taking in the blue skies and balmy weather but signally failing to derive any joy from what he saw.

'I do hope you're not going to turn all crotchety on me.'

'No, ma'am. Of course not, ma'am.'

'Very good.' She nodded, dismissively, turning back to her paper.

While it was true that the Queen was quite passionate about horses, there was a particular reason why that headline had caught her eye that particular day: she was due to host a lunch for her racing adviser and several trainers. She was doing so not in her capacity as head of state, but as one of the country's most enthusiastic thoroughbred breeders and racers.

Within days of joining the royal family, I'd become aware of Her Majesty's keen involvement in every aspect of her race-horses' lives. She owned many, and her racing colours, inherited from her father and great grandfather, King Edward VII, were a purple and scarlet jacket with gold braiding and a black cap. Her horses had won hundreds of races, including most of the British Classics.

The Queen wasn't a gambler; her own fascination was with bloodlines and breeding, with her own horses foaled at the Royal Stud on her Sandringham estate. She would follow the progress of each one of these, and while I had yet to accompany her on one of these visits, Winston and Margaret told me they were always enjoyable because Her Majesty was so happy to return to the equine world, where she wasn't automatically the centre of attention, and with beings who didn't pay her any deference because she was the Queen.

That day's lunch with the racing fraternity was one of easy informality. The guests were all long-standing friends and colleagues, and from the moment they arrived there was a convivial buzz, Her Majesty taking evident pleasure from the banter that went on around the table. It was only because this was a private occasion that I was allowed to be present in the Queen's own dining room, a more intimate affair than the grand chambers used for state occasions. An Indian rug by the window was the perfect spot to follow everything that went on. Begging for titbits from Her Majesty's guests would, I intuited, result in my instant banishment.

The forthcoming season's calendar was discussed, focusing on the health and training performance of the various horses. There were anecdotes from Sandringham, stories about other owners and trainers and mention of a visit the Queen had made to Kentucky years ago to leading Bluegrass horse farms.

Talk turned to jockeys and who was being considered for some of the key races. One jockey was said to be struggling with his weight. The confidence of another was said to have suffered after he'd taken a tumble the year before. Athletic fitness and horsemanship were also mentioned.

'So much to consider,' the Queen mused at one point. 'I wonder what you might say is *the* most important factor for success?'

'*The* most?' repeated Cameron, her racing adviser, a lofty, distinguished-looking man who was, every inch of him, the aristocrat.

'For my money,' ventured one of Her Majesty's trainers, the tweed-clad Ross from Hampshire, 'it would have to be impulse control.'

There was a pause while the others digested his reply, before a few nodded around the table.

'I'd agree,' concurred Armstrong, a large, jolly man who was another of Her Majesty's trainers. 'When you consider all that's required – the training for physical strength, the high level of fitness, the very strict diet to keep weight down, then the actual training with horses – all of those demand exceptional self-discipline.'

'Emotional intelligence, I believe they call it these days, ma'am,' said Cameron.

'They do?'

'Apparently it's a more accurate predictor of success in later life than straightforward intelligence. Having a high IQ is no guarantee of later fulfilment. But the ability to defer short-term gratification for the sake of a much greater prize seems to be what separates the sheep from the goats, so to speak.'

'How interesting.'

I was to learn that even though Her Majesty spoke plainly, her tone of voice communicated a hundred different nuances of meaning. 'How interesting' was a phrase she often used, but depending *how* she said it, it could mean anything from 'do, please, tell me more' to 'you are boring me to tears, I do wish you would shut up'.

In this particular case, both voice and bright-eyed enquiry communicated keen interest.

'The theory came about when some faculty staff at Harvard University did a study on their own children. A group of them were given marshmallows by their teacher. They were told that the teacher was leaving the room. Any child who hadn't eaten the marshmallow when the teacher returned would be rewarded with a second.

'Some kids ate their marshmallow immediately.'

There were chuckles around the table.

'Some folded their arms and resolutely waited till the teacher got back. Others agonised, picking up the marshmallows, sniffing them, trying their hardest to resist temptation.

'Where things got interesting was that several decades later, a researcher found the results of the experiment and decided to follow up on the children, who were all quite some way into adulthood. What they found was that those children who had been better able to resist temptation went on to achieve far more with their lives than those who hadn't. Backing up –' he gestured '– Mr Ross's point about impulse control.'

'Hmm.' The Queen glanced over to where I was sitting, face between my front paws and my two back legs stretched back behind me, listening to the conversation. I wondered where her thoughts were leading her. Was it to the moment my atavistic urges had got the better of me that morning and I'd tugged free of Detective Lewis, desperate to herd the ducks into the pond? Or to the moment she had paused outside Palace Newsagency to discover what, precisely, had caused the equestrian world to be reduced to a state of shock?

'I think I might have eaten one of those marshmallows,' she admitted. 'Only this morning, we were reminded how difficult it is to reign in our impulses.'

Her Majesty's guests didn't know quite what to make of this enigmatic statement, but that was hardly surprising. I had no doubt she was saying it for my benefit.

'Is this impulse control something one develops early on?' she wanted to know.

'Mostly,' said Cameron. 'The encouraging thing is that EQ, or willpower, can be developed at any time in life. But one needs a strong sense of motivation. Some would say you need to be "goal driven".'

Her Majesty wrinkled her nose momentarily. 'Such an ugly phrase,' she said. 'It seems a little desperate. And usually quite self-centred. One thinks of the brave people who fight against the odds for wider causes.'

A far-away look came into the Queen's eye. 'Like one's father, for instance. His stammer. Overcoming that required a great deal of effort.'

There were murmurs of sympathetic agreement from around the table.

'Perhaps a better phrase,' she continued, 'might be "a sense of purpose".'

'Indeed, ma'am!' Cameron was enthusiastic.

'A strong sense of purpose is what inspires one to strive to overcome obstacles and reach a particular objective.'

Although the conversation had started on the subject of jockeys, it had broadened considerably. And there could be little doubt that Her Majesty wasn't speaking in hypothetical terms alone. She was, rather, offering a rare, personal insight.

'The great challenge,' said Armstrong, 'is discovering what that personal purpose might be. Most people are so caught up in their busy lives they never give the matter much thought.'

'It's not something that someone else can tell you,' observed Cameron to general agreement. 'You have to work it out for yourself.'

'I'd even say,' continued Armstrong, 'that many people don't believe there *is* any purpose to life, beyond taking pleasure wherever you can find it.'

'Another day, another dollar,' said another trainer.

'He who dies with the most toys wins,' wisecracked Ross.

The pathos of the conversation was reflected on the Queen's face. 'One of the great privileges of my position is knowing that wealth, or "toys", are not an enduring source of contentment. Some of the most miserable people I know are amongst the most wealthy and powerful in the world. It's a great pity when people find themselves distracted by things that don't have any real meaning, when the things that could give their lives real purpose pass them by.'

'But would you agree, ma'am,' asked Cameron, 'that purpose is something for each one of us to find? That there's no ready-made formula?'

'Only up to a point.' Her Majesty was firm. 'We all have our own temperaments and interests. Our natural abilities are all quite different. What matters is what we do with them. I have learned over the years that the most fulfilled and purposeful people are those who have turned their abilities to a cause that's greater than themselves. Whether it is a brilliant research scientist seeking a cure for illness, or an elderly pensioner working in a charity mailing room, there is always the same application of energy for the greater good.'

Around the table there wasn't so much a murmur as a clamour of agreement.

'I would like to hear you say that on TV,' said Cameron.

'Your next Christmas message?' offered Ross.

Her Majesty smiled. 'I don't know. People don't like being lectured to. More important to show with actions than with words, don't you think? To lead by example.'

Household staff arrived to clear empty plates. Sorbets were produced as palate-cleansers.

The Queen turned to Cameron. 'Returning to impulse control, what exactly can be done to develop more of it? It seems to me this would be very useful, and not only for our jockeys.'

'Indeed, ma'am. There are a number of things that support strong impulse control. Having plenty of sleep is one of them – when people are tired, they're more vulnerable to temptation. Nutrition is another. When we're hungry, our will is weakened.'

'That's why diets never work!' offered the portly Armstrong to general merriment. 'I speak from experience!'

'There is great truth in that,' concurred Cameron. 'It is also said that order is contagious. If we live and work in an orderly way, it becomes easier to take control of more and more elements of our life. The opposite is also true. Chaos, stress and having demands constantly made on us clouds our focus and makes impulse control much less likely.'

'The constant ringing of mobile phones,' said Ross.

There were groans of recognition from around the table. Once again, Her Majesty looked over in my direction: yes, we both knew about the impact of a mobile phone ringing at the wrong moment.

'It's troubling how much time people spend on them,' observed the Queen. 'Especially the young ones.'

'They are degrading people's attention spans,' agreed Armstrong, emphatically. 'Heavy users are less able to recall things, and more easily distracted.'

There was a discussion about the stress created by mobile devices, how the boundary between work and leisure time had become blurred, and how people's peace of mind was directly affected.

'Technology is supposed to be our benefit, not the other way around,' observed Cameron. 'If there was ever a case of the tail wagging the dog, this has to be it.'

'Better the dog had no tail,' agreed Her Majesty, as her lunch guests joined her in turning to look at me.

Leaping up, I hurried over to where she was sitting, my stump twitching with vigour.

The lunch guests had departed and the Queen was returning upstairs when she heard a muffled sob echo down the corridor. I followed on her heels as she headed in the direction of the noise. Around a corner we discovered Detective Lewis standing forlornly outside Huchens' office.

As soon as Her Majesty honed into view, the police woman snapped to a more upright posture, hurriedly wiping her eyes with the back of her hand.

'What's the matter?' asked the Queen.

'I'm to be interviewed about this morning's security lapse, ma'am. I was told –' her voice cracked '– it was the worst breach in years. I don't know how I can begin to apologise.'

'That's not necessary,' the Queen said briskly. 'I'm still alive and well. Your bleeping phone distracted you?'

'Yes, ma'am.'

'An important message?'

No, ma'am. Not at all. Just an alert.'

'Alert?'

'For my next Scrabble move.'

Her Majesty frowned, 'As in the game?'

'Yes, ma'am.'

'On your phone?'

Detective Lewis removed the phone from her pocket. 'I am playing someone in Rio de Janeiro.'

'Gracious!' The Queen was intrigued. 'Do show me.'

Little was Detective Lewis aware that Her Majesty was keen on Scrabble. Not only an enthusiast, as it happened, but a seasoned player. Opening the app on her device, Detective Lewis began showing the Queen the online version of the game that had proved such a distraction that morning. She pointed out the arrangement on the board so far. The tiles from which she had to create her next word. How moves were indicated to one's remote partner by a signal such as the one that had been so dangerous earlier on.

She was still answering the Queen's questions when Huchens' door opened.

'Your Majesty,' he greeted her, his large and solid form filling the entrance.

'Detective Lewis here has been explaining why her phone went off. Most interesting.'

Huchens glanced from the Queen to the plainclothes policewoman with a poker face.

Her Majesty nodded briefly. 'I won't detain you,' she said, and headed towards a staircase. 'Try equanimity,' she instructed Detective Lewis.

'Ma'am?'

'Using the 'Q' on the top right-hand side. You've got all the letters. Double word score.'

'Yes, ma'am!' Detective Lewis's voice rose in astonishment. 'Thank you, ma'am!'

That evening, the Queen was visited by several family members. Charles, Camilla, Anne, William, Kate and Harry were joining Phillip and her for dinner. As they gathered in a sitting room, I made a beeline for Harry who, typically, was sitting on the floor. Throwing myself on the ground and rolling over, I was soon rewarded with a vigorous tummy rub.

'Had a good day, Gran?' enquired Harry.

'Went for a walk this morning with the puppy.' She nodded in my direction. 'It was such a nice morning.'

'Not one of your excursions?' asked Charles.

'Yes. The gardens.'

'Huchens would have been beside himself!'

'He was alright to begin with. But the puppy caught sight of some ducks and the girl holding him let go of his lead. There was quite a scene. Huchens marched me away.'

Her grandsons chuckled.

'Matters got worse, though. Huchens showed me down the pavement. He was going so dreadfully slowly that I stopped to read a magazine headline on the newsagent's stand. Something to do with a shock in the equestrian world. I wanted to find out what had happened. A nice Indian man popped out and gave it to me as a gift. He'd recognised me immediately.'

'Huchens must have been apoplectic!' exclaimed Charles.

'He was! When we got home he said he wanted to undertake –' at this point Her Majesty's entire being seemed to morph into the form of Huchens as she mimicked his heavily burring accent '– a full root and branch review.'

Everyone in the room burst out laughing. It was the first time I'd heard the Queen take off someone, and she was hilariously convincing.

'Did he tell you "the consequences would be catastrophic",' chuckled William, with his own Scottish riff.

'Not on this occasion.'

'You should have pushed him,' grinned Harry. 'Just that little bit more.'

'Leave the poor man alone,' said Her Majesty. 'He's only trying to do his job.'

The Queen went on to explain how the incident had been echoed by a discussion over lunch about impulse control. How she'd questioned her visitors about the qualities of a successful jockey and the idea of delaying gratification for a greater result was a theme that seemed to recur as a requirement for any form of achievement.

'In the military it's called G and D,' observed Harry. 'Guts and Determination.'

'Focus on the big picture,' agreed William.

'Although even military solutions can themselves be short-lived if they don't deliver a solution with which people will live,' pointed out Charles.

'Quite,' agreed Her Majesty. 'It always comes back to the point that actions must accord with values if they are to be meaningful.'

'And that the greatest value of all,' offered Charles, 'is the concern for the people and natural world around us.'

There was a pause while everyone of us in the room contemplated this profound point. Before Anne asked, 'By the way, Mummy, did you ever find out what it was that is shocking the equestrian world?'

'Oh!' the Queen was dismissive. 'Some hoo-ha at Ascot. Just the usual sensational headline leading to nothing at all.'

Philip, who had been dozing for most of the conversation, gathered himself up in his chair, jaw quivering and eyes fierce.

'Bloody journalists!' he exclaimed.

About a fortnight later, Tara was going through that day's mail.

'How did last night go?' Sophia asked from the other side of the office.

'You mean, with Richard at Rules?' confirmed Tara.

'I have high hopes this time,' said Sophia with a smile.

Tara fixed her with a droll expression. 'Well, I'm sorry to disappoint, but there won't be a weekend in Barcelona.'

'Why ever not?'

The possibility of Tara spending a long weekend with the man she had been dating for some weeks had been a source of much excited chatter between the two.

Tara frowned. 'I just found him irritating.'

'Like how?'

She shrugged. 'I can't say. Well, everything, really! He has this awful ring tone on his mobile that sets my teeth on edge every time it goes off.'

'I knew it!' Sophia's eyes blazed triumphantly. 'Just the same as the last guy. You didn't like the way he did his tie.'

'Well, it wasn't a Windsor knot!'

'And the man before, the soldier from Kent – what was that all about?'

'Yes, I know.' Tara grimaced. 'Hector halitosis.'

'You don't think that you're being just a little bit too picky?' asked Sophia.

'How can you kiss a man with a breath like smoked haddock?' she demanded, before turning her attention very deliberately back to the post.

A short while later, she had taken a greatly reduced pile of correspondence through to the Queen.

'This is my favourite for the day,' she said, handing over a copy of the latest edition of *Racing News*.

'Ah, the magazine I was given the other week from ...' Her Majesty waved her hand vaguely towards the back of the palace.

'Rajeev Sharma,' confirmed Tara. 'He's written a note with this one. Something along the lines that seeing you were so interested in the last issue of the magazine, it would be his honour to offer you a free annual subscription.'

'I see.'

The Queen glanced over to where Huchens was overseeing a routine bug-sweep of the offices. A subversive gleam appeared in her eye. 'Well,' she said, more loudly than she needed, 'that's kind of him, but I can't accept. Perhaps the two of us should pay him a visit. It's such a lovely afternoon. We can pay for the subscription.'

Huchens cleared his throat importantly. 'I would strongly advise against that, ma'am,' he rumbled, approaching where the Queen was sitting. 'We have no idea who this Sharma fellow is – *if* that's his real name. There's been no ID clearance. No premises check.'

'We could take the puppy,' proposed Tara, playing along with Her Majesty. 'I'm sure he'll be better behaved this time.'

Huchens colour was rapidly deepening.

'Good idea!' chimed the Queen.

'I'm sorry, but for security reasons I can't allow it!' Huchens' anguish at having to veto Her Majesty's plans was evident in his crimson cheeks.

'The consequences,' he declared, 'could be catastrophic!'

Four

Aquestion may well have arisen in your mind over the previous few chapters. Having established at the outset that my name is Nelson and that the Queen had me rescued as a puppy, you may very well be wondering how exactly the name and I became connected.

And why?

Am I called after that heroic figure of British naval history, Vice Admiral Horatio Nelson, who stands, to this day, atop a column in London's Trafalgar Square, just down the Mall from Buckingham Palace? Did Her Majesty detect in me a quality of inspiring leadership or strategic insight that made her think instantly of one of Britain's most illustrious figures? Or was there some other reason?

I could tell you that the reason I have been holding out on this particular tale is for reasons of chronological accuracy. It did take some months for me to be named, the feeling in the royal household being that doing things well is generally more important than doing them quickly. But historical accuracy wasn't the only or even most important reason for waiting until now.

When I think about what I've told you so far, I realise that my story is little other than a catalogue of failure. Urinating on the floorboards of Buckingham Palace. Breaking free of Her Majesty's security detachment, putting her very safety at risk. How would *you* like to be the subject of such embarrassing admissions?

Sadly, those tales are innocuous compared to the one I am about to relate. As a puppy – or in your case, child – you are forgiven the occasional indiscretion or lapse of judgment. You are still finding your way in the world. As an adolescent, however, you are expected to know better. You are supposed to show a bit of control, and, in royal circles, decorum. Your hormones may be kicking in but that's no excuse to behave like some crazed, rutting beast.

In my defence, I had no idea who Charles's visitor was that day. It shouldn't matter, of course, but in this case it does.

If that all sounds somewhat cryptic, my fellow subject, read on!

That particular weekend, Charles was corgi-sitting all three of us at Highgrove, his personal home in Gloucestershire, while the Queen was making a brief trip to Europe. Highgrove was always a treat for we three, having open access to gardens brimming with unfamiliar scents, astir with life. At mid-morning a visitor appeared with his own dog, a pretty, little white poodle called Mitzy. Charles and the visitor headed straight outside to walk through the sunlit gardens with an ease of familiarity suggesting that this was something of an established routine. All three of us corgis initially accompanied the men. But like Mitzy, we were soon embarking on our own adventures, distracted by powerful aromas beckoning from the flower beds, chasing each other down tunnels of sweet peas, scrambling excitedly at the sight of a distant rabbit.

It was quite some distance from the two men when I first noticed Mitzy, *really* noticed her. I was already earning a reputation for sociability, having befriended Football the cat while on holiday at Balmoral, and forming a close affection for one of the Queen's horses at Sandringham, who would bend down to greet me with a gentle nuzzle, something Her Majesty had remarked upon warmly.

The attraction I felt towards Mitzy, however, was of an altogether different kind. Admiring her fluffy rump, the way the saucy little minx thrust her hindquarters in the air while snuffling in the undergrowth, I was suddenly and powerfully overwhelmed by a new instinct: I had to have her!

Mitzy reacted to my brazen mounting at first with surprise, then with apparent willingness before turning, for no apparent reason, and nipping me. Yelping, I leapt from her, much to the droll amusement of Winston nearby – Margaret, fortunately, was still in relentless, if futile, pursuit of the trespassing hare.

Why did I attempt a second, third and even fourth mounting? I cannot say, without blaming hormones. And it was only the quite severe bite, and cautioning bark that followed, that saw me off. Mitzy headed back towards her owner. Reacting to the bark, the two men looked over at the approaching dogs.

'The new pup's probably taking liberties,' observed Charles, more accurately than he could have realized.

The two men chuckled.

Deciding that she'd be safest staying close to her owner, Mitzy remained almost to heel as we made our way into the Carpet Garden, a beautiful courtyard centred on a fountain, surrounded by cypresses, vines, oaks and orange trees in bloom.

'Quite, quite beautiful!' exclaimed Charles's visitor.

He was a middle-aged man, slight of build, with a receding hairline and a bespectacled, intelligent-looking face. There was a sparkle in his eyes as he took in his surroundings.

'"To feed the soil, warm the heart and delight the eye." Wasn't that your objective for Highgrove Gardens?' he confirmed.

Charles nodded. 'In this particular spot, we've tried to capture the Mediterranean ideal of the garden as heaven on earth.'

The visitor stood, taking everything in. 'Most people would feel much more harmony and peace if they could connect to the natural world more often. All those years I spent in corporate offices I used to think how cut off we were.'

'From nature?'

'Yes.' Then, after a pause, 'But not only from that. Many people had long commutes which meant they were pretty cut off from their family for a lot of the week. The relentless grind of it all would leave them exhausted by the weekend. There wouldn't be much time to recover, then the whole cycle would start all over again.'

As I nosed around the visitor, I wondered who he was. Could he be some high-flying business leader? Nothing in the scent of his walking shoes or freshly pressed trousers provided so much as a clue.

Mitzy remained very close to him – but always on the other side of his legs from me.

'It does seem that many people are having to work longer hours than ever before,' said Charles. 'And the impact of mobile devices …'

'Terrible!' The visitor was shaking his head. 'You no longer leave work at the office. It's in your pocket. Work time and personal time have become blurred.'

'And one often has the feeling that people are only half paying attention these days. Even when they put their phones onto silent, you see them react to the vibration in their pockets or handbags. They get distracted. You can tell that their thoughts have gone elsewhere.'

'It seems to me there's a great paradox,' said the visitor. 'People have never communicated so much with each other by phone and social media. But at the same time, we seem to be going backwards in our ability to be really present to each other.'

Charles tapped a nearby stone with his foot, thoughtfully, before saying, 'So many paradoxes, aren't there? Our society has never been so affluent. We've never had such amazing technology. Or travelled so much. Or had such long life expectancy. But along with all the good things is this dark underside. Depression affecting one in four people. The increase in single-person households and social fragmentation. On the one hand we're materially better off than ever. On the other, it doesn't seem to have made us any happier.'

Charles's visitor regarded him closely. 'I wrestle with exactly this dilemma all the time.'

Nodding, Charles began walking again, heading in the direction of the organic gardens surrounding the oak pavilion, a mysterious structure mounted with an obelisk that was nevertheless curiously in keeping with the lavish foliage and plants all around it.

'As a society, I often feel we're at risk of losing our way,' said his visitor. 'We've made it all about the individual. Glorification of the self. People feel under pressure to have a certain lifestyle. On social media kids feel under pressure to create these fictional personas to seem cool, more enviable, to have more online friends. At the same time, there's a recognition that it's all pointless make-believe. Which leads to profound unease.

'When I go to poorer countries, they are preoccupied by very different things. If your electricity supply is hit and miss, or you can't always buy rice or soap or toothpaste at the shops, you don't take anything for granted. You barter with friends. You rely on neighbours. There's a genuine inter-dependence, a sense of being connected. It brings people closer as a community, and that willingness to help each other out really makes people value each other.'

'Are you saying,' asked Charles, 'that our social problems have come about because people aren't deprived enough?'

Behind his glasses, his visitor's eyes twinkled with humour. 'That's a provocative question!'

'It's meant to be,' chuckled the Prince of Wales.

'I do sometimes wish I could put people on a plane to parts of Africa or South America for a few months. The change in kids who go overseas to volunteer in their gap year is usually quite remarkable.'

'I've seen it myself.'

'Gives them a completely different perspective. They come back more grounded. Resilient.'

'The benefit of a broader perspective.'

'Quite.'

For a while the two strolled towards the oak pavilion in silence before the visitor said, 'Going back to your question about our social problems, a lot of them have to do with affluenza.'

'Materialism?'

'Believing extrinsic things are more important to our happiness than they actually are,' agreed the visitor. 'And, by the same token, undervaluing the importance of non-material, intrinsic things.'

It was a pause before Charles said, 'How eloquently put. And, of course, that's not something I could ever say. Not in public, at least. People would just say, "He's being a hypocrite".' He fiddled with his cufflinks. 'Even though if anyone should know how little satisfaction wealth can bring, it's me.' He looked pensive for a while before he asked, 'What should the message be? What are the intrinsic things we should be encouraging?' He gave a droll smile. 'Telling people they should go to church more often?'

'Or even at all,' interjected his visitor with a wry chuckle. 'Sadly, for many people any form of organised religion has become irrelevant. If you believe you are nothing more than matter, which is the materialist view, then it is rational to dismiss spirituality. Persuading people that this is a tragically diminished idea of what it means to be human is, of course, our ultimate purpose. But even with a materialist mindset, we can encourage people to review their priorities.'

'Oh?' Charles sounded interested.

'For most people, what's meaningful are the things that draw us together. What we do with the people we care about. The communities we're a part of. It's about what connects us.'

'Hmm,' the Prince of Wales digested this. 'I've met a number of entrepreneurs over the years who say the most satisfying thing they did was return to the places where they grew up, sometimes quite deprived places, and help out the local sports team, or brass band, for example. It can be a deeply moving experience.'

'Exactly.' His visitor nodded. 'When we make positive connections, or reconnections with those who've helped us in the past, then we find purpose and well-being. Wealth and status actually become irrelevant.'

The two men were approaching the veranda when Margaret appeared on the lawn ahead of us, racing from one side to the other. Winston and I scampered after her. Too apprehensive to follow, Mitzy quivered at the ankles of her master in a state of bewildered perturbation.

It was a short while later, after Charles and his visitor had re-tired to a drawing room for tea, that I behaved in an unspeakable fashion. You know me well enough by now, my fellow subject, to realise that I am not one to sugar-coat things or to avoid an uncomfortable truth. But nor do I wish to dwell on unpleasantness, so I shall tell you what happened – just the once.

Charles was searching for a favourite book on one of his shelves as he and his visitor continued to talk about deep and meaningful subjects. Margaret and Winston remained out-side, savouring the delights of the garden. I, meantime, fol-lowing my instincts, found myself sitting at the feet of the visitor – Mitzy having hopped up onto the sofa beside him the moment I appeared.

I still had no idea who the visitor was. My initial view of him being a corporate leader had changed – his travels seemed more inclined to the cerebral, even the spiritual. As he and the Prince of Wales had an animated discussion about medicine in the developing world, I wondered if he was the head of one of the aid charities that Sophia talked about so often.

Even had I known who he was, I don't suppose it would have stopped me from obeying my instincts. Which I regret to say were of the basest possible kind. His trousers, which I had found to be so bland and lacking in olfactory interest when he'd first arrived were, by now, thoroughly permeated with the scent of Mitzy. A few, telltale white curls had been left behind by her on the fabric. Mitzy had placed herself up on the sofa, coquettish and unattainable. But the visitor's leg was pressed to the floor at what suddenly appeared to be a most interesting angle. Overwhelmed by the spell of Mitzy, her scent, her poodleness, her beguiling, fluffy rump, I couldn't help myself. In a trice I had mounted the leg of the Prince of Wales's visitor and began vigorous frottage.

It lasted only moments.

'Ugh!' protested the visitor. He shook his leg, and forced me off with a vigorous shove of the hand. I tumbled onto my side.

Turning back from his bookshelves, Charles instantly surmised what had happened. 'Good heavens!' he exclaimed.

'Bit frisky,' observed the visitor.

Charles raised an arm, pointed to the door and glowered at me. 'Out!' he ordered.

Embarrassed by my impetuousness, and ashamed to have disgraced myself in front of the heir to the throne, I made my cringing way out to the garden.

The very next morning, a short while after all three of we corgis had returned home to Windsor, Tara was attaching a lead to my collar and taking me outside. A walk in the park, I wondered? Or perhaps along the river? But what about Winston and Margaret? Were they not coming too?

Soon we were in her car and driving out the gates. The steel bars resplendent with the lion and the unicorn closed behind us as Tara headed into Windsor. The one and only time I'd been in her car had been when she'd rescued me from the Grimsleys. Since then I'd been on innumerable car journeys, but these had always been chauffeured by a royal driver or a police detective. What on earth was happening?

It was only when we turned down a particular street, passing a hairdressing salon which bloomed with a potent and unmistakable melange of scents, that I realised where we were going. Dr Munthe had examined me soon after coming under the care of the Queen, ensuring I'd had the required inoculations. A bearded man with a Swedish accent, he was famous for being a dog lover and I'd felt quite at ease when being taken to his surgery.

What surprised me was how, on this occasion, instead of waiting with me to go into see Dr Munthe, Tara left me with one of his nurses.

'I'll collect you this afternoon, young man,' she said, exchanging a knowing smile with a veterinary nurse. I was soon taken to a back room in which there were five kennels for dogs and, along one of the sides of the room, a number of smaller enclosures occupied by cats. Of the five, three were already occupied. An elderly Alsatian, his leg in plaster, was sleeping in the corner kennel. Next to him a wheezing, middle-aged Labrador wagged her tail limply as I appeared. A King Charles spaniel was in the kennel next to the one into which I was guided – but he was in the deepest of sleeps.

The nurse crouched down and gave me a reassuring pat. 'Won't be long.'

I dimly remember being taken into a room where Dr Munthe checked my temperature and gave me a quick examination. A needle must have been involved somewhere because, without even noticing, I fell into the deepest of sleeps.

The next thing I remember is opening my eyes to find myself looking into what could have been a mirror, but was none other than Jasper – my same-litter oldest brother! He now occupied the cage beside mine, which had been empty when I'd arrived.

'Never thought I'd see you again, Number Five!' He extended his tongue between the bars of our cages. My eyelids were so heavy I had to close them again. As I did, I felt his warm lick and scent – along with a rush of recognition.

'What's going on?' I asked drowsily. I felt a sense of deep peace. I was being greeted by a much-loved being from the distant past. Was this the fabled Rainbow Bridge? Had I crossed to the place they called 'the other side'?

I was mulling over this dreamily, when Jasper said, 'You've been fixed.'

At the time, the word meant nothing to me.

'Both of us have,' he continued. 'Same day. Same vet. What are the chances?!'

It took all my energy to blink my eyes open again. 'Fixed?' I asked. 'What's that?'

'Fixed? Neutered. De-sexed. Castrated. Had your balls chopped off.'

'Doesn't sound good,' I mused.

'Depends.' His tone was sanguine. 'It can get rid of an unwanted distraction.'

Just as I remembered, my brother still had a reassuring air about him. The last time I had seen Jasper, he was at the end of a lead being taken to the park by Mrs Grimsley. I also remembered the special bond that had grown up between us in those final few days we'd spent together. How it had been Jasper, more than anyone, who had taken my mind off the constant threat of the shed. The simple fact of his amiable presence had been deeply reassuring then, just as it was now that we were both older.

After a while he cocked his head and fixed me with a mischievous expression. 'Was it something in particular that brought you here, Number Five? Misbehaving at home?'

Perhaps it was the anaesthetic that blurred my short-term memory. 'Oh, no,' I told him, with sleepy confidence. 'Very well-behaved.'

'You sure?' He seemed unconvinced. 'You haven't been jumping on other dogs? Dry-humping anyone?'

Oh.

No sooner had he mentioned it, than the image of the drawing room at Highgrove came to mind. The Prince of Wales's visitor with the tempting little vixen beside him on the sofa. The regrettable incident. Charles's pointed arm and red face and my disgraced retreat. So that was why I had been taken to the vet!

But how did Jasper know?

'Humans don't like it,' he continued. 'Especially the posh ones like yours.'

Starting to feel more properly awake, I wondered how he seemed to know so much about me. 'Why are you so perky?'

'I've had half an hour longer in recovery than you. You'll also be wide awake soon.' He shifted his body to one side. 'If somewhat tender.' Suddenly his ears were pricked up and eyes bright with interest. 'So tell me, are you really the Queen's favourite corgi?'

'It's not like that,' I told him. 'There's also Winston and Margaret.'

'You live at Buckingham Palace?'

'Part of the time.'

I could tell that he wanted to know more – but I had questions of my own. 'How do you know about me?

'It's all over the Kennel Club!' he said. 'Ever since you joined the royal family the Grimsleys haven't stopped talking about it. Desdemona is a show corgi who belongs to my family's cousins. She comes back from meetings full of stories.'

'Like?'

'Like how the Grimsleys now transport their corgis in red and gold carriers, and put them in red and gold collars and show them with red and gold leashes. How Mrs Grimsley wears gloves and hats like the Queen and when they arrive at Kennel Club meetings she waves at people like she's in the royal carriage on her way to Westminster Abbey. They've become very hoity toity,' said Jasper, 'since they got the Royal Warrant.'

Still feeling somewhat woozy, I wondered if I'd heard him right. 'Warrant?'

'Desdemona says they have the coat of arms plastered all over the place. They even have a car pennant.'

'But ... there *is* no warrant,' I told him.

'What?' Despite his post-operative state, Jasper pushed himself up on his front legs in surprise.

'And they'll never get one.'

'You sure?' He was scandalised, his large, pink tongue lolling out of his mouth.

'They never, knowingly, supplied the royal family with anything. In fact, they demanded total secrecy.'

I observed the bewilderment on Jasper's face, before saying, 'Let me tell you the story.'

You know better than anyone, my fellow subject, the tale of what happened that fateful afternoon in Slough was not an edifying one. But being able to explain the whole thing to my brother came as a curiously unexpected relief. Of course the Queen's ladies-in-waiting knew what had happened, as did Her Majesty, in summary version. My fellow royal corgis had also heard the exchanges between Tara and Sophia. But none of them really *knew* what it was like to live with the Grimsleys – not like Jasper. We had been through the same puppyhood together and being able to share the story of those final few hours in Slough, and my subsequent journey to Windsor, was wonderfully cathartic.

Jasper understood. He got it.

He was also scandalised by the Grimsleys' claims. Within weeks, he assured me, every dog at the Kennel Club would know the truth about the matter, even if none of the humans did.

At least, not yet.

Then he was telling me about his own adoptive family. How Ronnie Bowers, the ten-year-old boy who had pleaded with his parents for months to have a dog, was the best companion a corgi could possibly have, and how they went for long rambles in the countryside. How Mrs Bowers' sister had connected the family to the Grimsleys, being a corgi enthusiast and owner of Desdemona. Apart from being a distant and prize-winning relative, Desdemona was also a conduit of family news.

Through her, Jasper had heard that our mother, still living under the kitchen sink, was heavily pregnant with another litter of pups. Tarquin, long the alpha-male of the household, was suffering from a touch of rheumatism. Meanwhile, an American heiress had made an offer to buy Annabelle.

As Jasper passed on news of all the beings, both corgi and human, who had been my whole world in the early days, the feeling of connection I had to him grew even stronger. Even the way he called me 'Number Five' was delightfully nostalgic.

'You know, Jasper,' I told him through the cage bars, 'I never had the chance to say thank you for all you did for me back in Slough.'

'Didn't do anything.' He seemed genuinely mystified.

'You cheered me up. It was a scary time for me, you know, with the shed.'

'We'll never know what happens in there.' Even now, he was a determined optimist.

'No corgi ever came back,' I reminded him.

'No.' He re-adjusted his hindquarters somewhat gingerly. 'But things turned out alright for you in the end, didn't they?'

'Couldn't be better.'

'You won't want to be seen with the likes of me anymore.'

'Don't be silly.'

'You, the Queen's Corgi. Me, inescapably middle class.'

I was suddenly reminded of what Charles's visitor had said so recently in the drawing room at Highgrove. 'Just a few days ago a visitor was saying how by making positive reconnections, especially with those who've helped us in the past, we can find purpose and well-being. How wealth and status become irrelevant.'

'Who was the visitor?'

'Don't know.'

Brown eyes gleaming, Jasper could tell I wasn't being entirely forthcoming. He stretched his paw between the bars and pressed mine.

'Actually, it was the one whose leg I ...'

He grinned widely. 'An Earl or a Duke or some such?'

'Could be. But the family don't just see people with pedigrees. They entertain all sorts. Even bitsas. I still don't know who that one was. Do you think it's important?'

'Who knows?' He looked away.

I knew that gesture – Jasper's way of avoiding a particular truth.

So it *did* matter. But who was the mild-manner man with the cerebral air – and the fluffy white temptress? And why was the thought of her now suddenly so devoid of temptation? And was this how it was going to be for the rest of my life?

Pulling me from my thoughts Jasper said, 'You still haven't told the most important thing, Number Five?'

'Which is?'

'Your name. What does the Queen call you?'

'Nothing at the moment. She didn't want to rush into things. They're waiting for something to suggest itself. Some particular event.'

Jasper's mouth broke open and stump wagged.

'What's so funny?'

'You know what that event is going to be, don't you?'

It took me a moment to catch on. 'Surely not!'

'You said the other two are called Margaret and Winston. Hmm. Which head of state is a notorious philanderer?'

'That's not the way it works.' I knew it was only brotherly teasing, but I just couldn't help rising to the bait.

'I think you might find yourself called –'

'Her Majesty likes to find the good in people,' I interrupted.

'Lucky for you!' Jasper's eyes twinkled.

Everything was business as usual when I returned to Windsor, in the back of Tara's car. The royal family and their household staff were busy preparing for a banquet that evening in honour of the Czech president. Margaret, especially vigilant on such occasions, trotted through the corridors with an air of great busyness. But Winston, having noted my absence, took one look at me and instantly deduced what had happened.

'Ah, *The Snip*,' he said, in a sympathetic tone. 'I remember it well.'

'You do?'

'Many moons ago.'

'And how is it, afterwards?'

'No discomfort at all after a couple of days.'

'I mean, not having balls?'

Winston paused to consider this for a while. 'Quieter, dear boy. Calmer waters.'

'Your feeling of corgi-hood wasn't destroyed?' With Winston I knew I could ask such questions.

'Lord, no!' He glanced at me, concerned I should even be thinking such a thing. 'Wasn't it Sophocles,' he mused, 'who said that freedom from libido was like escaping from bondage to a madman?'

'Sophocles?' I asked, casting my mind back to the stables at Sandringham. 'One of the Queen's geldings?'

'Greek philosopher,' replied Winston. 'Apart from that thought, I know nothing about him. But it's a useful one, no?'

In the days that followed, the wound from my surgery healed and I discovered myself to be much the same corgi I had been before. Although one thing continued to bother me – the identity of the man whose leg I had mounted. It hadn't been my proudest moment. In fact, it was probably my least proud moment as a royal corgi. No reference had been made to it in my presence, but if Charles had said anything to the Queen, it didn't seem to have changed her affectionate manner towards me. All the same I couldn't help wondering.

When I asked Margaret if she knew the identity of Charles's guest, she claimed to have been far too busy fending the estate from the predations of rabbits to notice such a thing. Winston claimed age and forgetfulness. I had thought it would remain one of life's great mysteries unless, of course, the same man made a return visit.

And then, one day all three of us were in the staff kitchen, having just eaten dinner, when the man's face appeared on TV news.

'That's him!' I told Winston.

'Who?'

'Charles's visitor.'

There were the ascetic features, the receding, fair hair, the playful expression in his eyes.

'Ah, yes,' nodded Winston in recognition.

Was it my feeling of warm contentment with a tummy full of food, or the fact that I'd spent most of that afternoon curled up with Winston at Her Majesty's feet, cocooned in a state of safe well-being? Whatever the reason, I felt the impulse to confess. 'He was the one whose leg I jumped on,' I told Winston. 'Before being fixed.'

He regarded me closely.

'I think it was what I did that led to me being, you know –' I knew I was rambling '– sent to the vet.'

'You're serious?' There was merriment in his aged eyes. He jerked his head towards the TV. 'Justin?'

'Who's Justin?'

Winston never had to tell me, my fellow subject. I discovered for myself just seconds later when the scene changed to show Charles's visitor inside a cathedral wearing very different attire – golden robes and a gold-coloured hat, he was carrying a staff with an elaborate gold handle. Organ music blasted triumphantly as the newsreader said, 'The Archbishop of Canterbury announced last week …'

When I looked back at Winston his mouth was open in a broad smile.

'That's a first for a royal corgi,' he told me, the amusement of it becoming so great that he succumbed to a fit of snorting.

'I think you have a great career ahead of you, dear boy,' he told me, when he had fully recovered. 'Just not in the Church of England.'

My embarrassing encounter with the Archbishop of Canterbury couldn't have been further from my mind when, several weeks later, Her Majesty and the Prince of Wales made a private visit to a long-standing family friend at his farm in Gloucestershire.

As a royal corgi schooled in discretion – a claim I realise may be hard to accept given the shameful admission of this chapter – I can't reveal the identity of the friend except to say that he is a peer of the realm with a great interest in pedigree cattle.

After tea that afternoon, the whole party set out to admire a prize-winning dairy bull which the Lord had only recently acquired. They included the Queen, Charles, the lord and his lady, we three royal corgis and the lord's dog, Cara. A 12 year old golden retriever, Cara spent most of her days indoors and, when she moved, did so slowly on account of being almost completely blind. We had already exchanged warm wet nosed greetings before sniffing one another's backsides as canine etiquette dictates.

'It's amazing she doesn't bump into things,' Charles observed as she followed us out of the house.

'Familiarity,' explained the Lord. 'She's been through each barn and paddock on the estate nearly every week for the past 12 years.'

While this was true, Cara's almost complete lack of vision meant that when we all gathered next to a white palisade fence, unlike everyone else who stopped to observe the great, black bull grazing on the other side, Cara slipped under a cross bar and walked directly into the field, which was usually occupied only by placid heifers.

Cara's creeping deafness meant that when her master called for her to return, she heard him only dimly. She paused momentarily, turning in our direction, before continuing across the field directly towards where the bull had stopped grazing, eyeing the unwelcome visitor with evident displeasure.

His Lordship shouted out for Cara at the very top of his voice. But he only unsettled the bull further.

'I'll have to go in,' he declared urgently, bending to squeeze between the bars of the fence.

'Are you quite sure?' Her Majesty asked, concerned.

'I'll try to distract him while we get Cara out.'

Tension mounted as His Lordship, now on the other side of the fence, walked across the field, preparing to take on the bull from a different direction. The bull wasn't in the slightest bit interested. It seemed that a distant human was of far less concern than the approaching dog.

The bull was bending its neck towards the ground, glowering at Cara.

'Oh, goodness!' cried Her Ladyship. 'We know what that means!'

Clambering on the fence, she cried out to Cara with all her might. To no avail.

The bull raised its head high before bringing it heavily towards the ground again. A warning most dogs would have heeded. But Cara continued dawdling towards him.

Suddenly I felt a rush of those same herding instincts which had had me round up the ducks in Buckingham Palace Gardens. In a trice I was under the horizontal bar of the palisade fence and scampering towards Cara. A chorus of voices followed. The Queen sounded anxious. Charles imploring. I ignored them all, driven not only by instinct but also remembering, in that moment, what the Archbishop had said about inter-dependence and being willing to help others. Was I not doing the right thing? I continued steadily towards Cara.

Seeing a second canine intrude in its paddock, the bull grew livid. It raised and lowered its head more vigorously than before. It raised its front, right hoof and began scuffing. As I caught up with Cara for the first time it bellowed.

Hearing the blood-curdling sound, and so unexpectedly close, Cara froze.

Moments later I was next to her. She felt me touch her now-trembling leg with my snout and quickly re-establish a connection.

For what felt like the longest time there was a tense stand off, the bull regarding the two of us with frozen fury. His Lordship, having approached from another angle, halted in his tracks. I guided Cara with my nose back in the direction of the small group of people and corgis watching from the other side of the field.

I led the retreat, slowly, quietly. Not wishing to provoke the bull with precipitous action, I nuzzled Cara at a deliberate pace away from the great beast. From the corner of my eye, I saw His Lordship do much the same thing, taking steady steps backwards.

And, as soon as we were at a safer distance, I picked up the pace.

'Close call,' I barked as we headed back to the white palisades.

'How far away was the bull?' yapped Cara.

'I could see the veins of its eyes,' said I, with only the lightest touch of melodrama.

There was huge relief and many warm words spoken on our return.

'What a brave little chap!' Her Ladyship was effusive in her thanks, patting me warmly.

'He's only new to the household, but he's already making his mark,' agreed the Queen.

Margaret, to her credit, greeted me back like a triumphant general home from some distant islands protecting the realm. Winston wagged his stump with pride.

'You fought them in the fields!' said he.

'What an amazing pup!' exclaimed His Lordship when he'd returned to the group. Crouching down, he put both my front paws on his thigh and proceeded giving me a vigorous, two-handed rubbing.

'He doesn't have a name yet,' said Her Majesty. 'We have been waiting for something to suggest itself.'

'Well, Your Majesty, I think something just has! Heaven knows what could have happened to Cara in there if he hadn't gone to her rescue.'

The aged retriever was milling through everyone's legs, wagging her feathery tail gratefully.

'He's a brave diplomat' Her Ladyship enthused.

'So it seems,' the Queen was patting me, delighted.

'And very friendly,' His Lordship continued.

'If sometimes a little over-familiar,' contributed the Prince of Wales with a chuckle.

The Queen met his eye with a cautioning glance. But as their eyes met, they seemed to hold for a moment.

'Are you thinking what I'm thinking?' asked Charles.

'About a name?' confirmed Her Majesty, her smile broadening.

He nodded. 'I think we have it!' he beamed. Then glancing at the gathered throng, 'My Lord and Lady, Cara, Winston and Margaret, I give you the newest member of the royal family, Nelson!'

'Horatio?' queried His Lordship.

At the same time that Her Ladyship chimed, 'Mandela?'

Everyone turned to Her Majesty for a definitive answer.

'Well,' she said, after considering this for a moment. 'Couldn't it be a bit of both?'

Five

News that the Queen's littlest corgi now had a name began to circulate through the royal residences. And along with the name, the story behind it. My rescue of Cara, and how I'd herded her away from danger was repeated and embellished. Everyone from Her Majesty's private secretary to security's German shepherds were made aware of my finest hour. I was no longer an un-named newcomer, one whose qualities – apart from a floppy ear – had yet to be discerned. Instead I was becoming known as a corgi of courage and friendliness. Still getting used to the novelty of having a name at all, in those first few days after the visit to his Lordship, I felt a thrill of satisfaction every time I was summoned.

The Prince of Wales, in that deliberate voice of his, would linger over the first syllable of my name. William and Harry would beckon me in brisk, playful tones. As for the Queen, from the very first time she called me, she did so in distinctive two tone, the second syllable of my name very much higher than the first: 'Nel-*son!*'

For the first time in my life I truly belonged.

Not that it was allowed to go to my head. There were still occasional wisecracks about the Archbishop of Canterbury's leg when we were taken on walks by security. Any reference to the Church of England, cathedrals or priests might provoke a sideways glance in my direction from Margaret. And even though, as a neutered corgi, the notion of wanting to mount any person's leg – or, indeed, any poodle – was now entirely academic, I still remembered my moment of shame with a heavy heart.

Even my rescue of Cara was soon placed well and truly into context. A couple of weeks after the visit to his Lordship, we three corgis found ourselves accompanying Her Majesty on a brief visit to an agricultural centre in Berkshire. It was a visit we had known about for weeks in advance and had been awaiting with the keenest curiosity. But nothing quite prepared us for the spectacle we were to see.

All three of us were used to the idea of professional canines. Indeed, we regarded ourselves as being in service to the Queen. What was Winston, if not a font of wisdom and forbearance – though not always in the case of canapés? Meantime, a single raised lip of Margaret's was all it now needed for a potential garden party pilferer to think better of filling their pockets with cucumber sandwiches, or indeed, dainty items from the patisserie. Still a pup, I was evolving my own brand of affectionate diplomacy.

The amateur nature of the royal corgis' well-meaning efforts, however, became crystal clear on that memorable afternoon. We followed Her Majesty as she emerged from an unmarked police car to be greeted by the tweed-clad organising committee of the English National Sheepdog Trials. The Queen made a point of taking our leashes personally as she was shown to a dais under a white marquee overlooking large, open fields. There was a murmur of amusement as we three followed, walking obediently to heel, to the centre of the small platform where Her Majesty sat, with several other guests of honour, among a group of about forty people. To her right was a man of aristocratic bearing, introduced to her as the Chairman of the English National Sheepdog Trials. To her left was a dark-haired woman with a broad smile who needed no introduction at all.

The Queen watches very little television. Quite apart from a busy calendar of official duties, her evenings are mostly taken up with her family life and circle of close friends. But there are one or two television shows she thoroughly enjoys, and which her staff make sure are recorded for the rare occasions when she has time to relax. One of the shows, dealing with problematic canine behaviour, was hosted by none other than the woman beside her, whose hand she shook most warmly. It so happened, that the show was also one known to dogs throughout the world and we corgis, having watched so many of the programs, already felt on the friendliest of terms with the woman herself. Royal protocol forbids me from disclosing her identity, but let's just say that she shared her first name with a very long-serving monarch, only a few generations back in the family tree from the Queen herself. And she is widely known for her *positive* training.

The sheepdog trials were already well underway by the time we had arrived. Although Winston had attended one of these events in his puppyhood, for both Margaret and me it came as a revelation. We watched intently as border collies raced across the fields herding large flocks of sheep this way and that, guiding an ever-changing shape of furry bodies in whichever direction they were asked. On command, they would quite effortlessly divide small groups of sheep and guide them into separate enclosures, all the while following the instructions relayed to them by shepherds with nothing more than a slight bend of the body or gesture of the arm.

Within a few minutes, I came to realise that my rescue of poor, blind Cara had been a very modest affair compared with the spectacular manoeuvres I was now observing. And Margaret no doubt also realised that rounding up the occasional, errant trade unionist was small beer compared to the dazzling mastery on display now.

We watched, spellbound, the occasional human member of the audience unable to suppress a cry of encouragement or delight as his or her sheepdog performed some complex routine. One of the border collies, Flash, was especially mesmerising to watch, being both as swift as his name suggested, as well as smoothly adept in separating groups of sheep. He also seemed to have a developed sense of humour, sometimes springing over the moving bodies of his charges, giving the impression he was on both sides of them at once. He also prompted a round of chuckles when he rolled on the ground several times, all the while keeping intense watch on both the sheep and his master. Her Majesty seemed delighted by him and from the warmth of the applause that followed his performance it seemed that he was one of the favourites on the trial circuit.

As we sat overlooking that field in Berkshire, there seemed something quite inspiring about watching humans and canines working together, an invisible but powerful bond between them, continuing a tradition of working the land together that had been with us since time immemorial.

During a break in proceedings, Her Majesty stood to ease her legs. The positive dog lady proposed that the royal corgis would benefit from a short stroll – a suggestion to which the Queen readily agreed.

'I do hope you'll join us,' she said.

A short while later, all five of us, flanked by security, were making our way along the perimeter of the paddock.

'I like your TV show very much,' the Queen told the dog trainer.

All three of us were walking to heel, Her Majesty holding our leashes in her right hand. We were deeply curious to tune into this conversation.

'Thank you! Thank you, Your Majesty,' the other replied, smiling appreciatively.

'You offer sensible advice.'

'I can tell you do not need it,' she answered, gesturing towards us. 'When you walked from the car earlier, I could see immediately that you have a good relationship with the corgis.'

'Oh, yes!'

I glanced up at the Queen. And was it my imagination, or had she coloured slightly in the cheeks? 'What would you say is the most important element of dog training?'

'Without a doubt, positive reinforcement. If we want to build lasting bonds based on mutual trust and love, we need to embrace what we learn from behavioural science.'

The Queen listened thoughtfully. 'That hasn't always been the approach has it?'

'Unfortunately not!' The positive trainer was shaking her head. 'There have been so many myths repeated unquestioningly in the media about how all dogs are like wolves following pack behaviour. How they are constantly trying to assert dominance over us. Many people don't understand that training based on that model is actually hugely damaging. I spend a lot of time rescuing people's relationships with pets who have been subjected to dominance and punishment based trainers. Their methods go completely against positive human-animal bonding.'

The Queen was nodding. 'Yes, we know much more about animal behaviour today than we did even ten or twenty years ago.'

'Exactly. We have a better understanding of how dogs experience the world through their senses, and how they communicate using body language. Knowing better how their minds work and what emotions they experience, opens up a whole, new dimension of possibilities in the way we relate, once species to another.'

'On the subject of body language,' Her Majesty nodded in the direction of the open fields, 'very impressive performance by the border collies. It is intriguing how they know what to do with only the smallest signals from the shepherds.'

'A privilege to watch,' her companion agreed. 'Lots of training. Positive reinforcement.'

'And consistency?' confirmed the Queen.

'Absolutely! Dogs get very confused by inconsistent messages. Like if one family member lets them jump on the sofa, and another one doesn't. Sometimes it's even the same person changing their mind, depending on their mood. That leaves a dog bewildered about what is or isn't acceptable.'

Her Majesty was following this closely. 'And consistency also between what we say and what we do.'

'Exactly. Dogs are far more observant than humans when it comes to non verbal communication. If you say one thing to a dog, while physically indicating something different, chances are the dog will follow the non verbal direction.'

'The more authentic of the two.'

They walked a short distance further before the dog lady said, 'You could probably say that being consistent and authentic are the keys to successful training.'

'Not only that,' agreed the Queen, pausing for a moment. 'I believe they are the keys to happiness and purpose in every aspect of our lives.'

As we were returning to the marquee, I noticed there had been changes in the audience as owners came and went with their dogs. I was especially pleased to see, at the end of the front row sitting next to a tall, tanned man, none other than Flash. I wouldn't dream of trying to drag the Queen over towards him, of course. But as soon as she and the dog trainer had settled, the three of us back under their seats, I made my way surreptitiously under the front row of seats until I reached the end.

'Brilliant performance!' I told Flash with a wag of the stump.

He cocked his head modestly, suggesting it had all been in a day's work.

'Would you like to meet the Queen?' I felt sure she would like to congratulate him personally.

Flash obediently looked up at his owner, who glanced at where I had the sheepdog's leash between my teeth. He gave an amused shrug of consent.

In my own display of animal husbandry, I padded along in front of the VIPs, still holding Flash's leash, while he followed a few steps behind. Reaching the centre, I dropped the leash at the feet of the Queen.

She exchanged an amused glance with the positive trainer. 'Thank you for the introduction, Nelson,' she murmured, before reaching out to Flash. 'You did very well, young man. A pleasure to watch.'

She stroked his neck, while Flash wagged his tail appreciatively. Ever watchful of his owner, Flash tilted back his head, glancing along the front row of VIPs. Her Majesty also caught his owner's eye and nodded with a smile. Then, at some signal almost imperceptible to me, he returned to his owner's side. I made my way under the Queen's seat.

'Very sociable,' said the dog trainer as I disappeared from view.

'Quite the diplomat,' agreed Her Majesty. 'Dogs, cats, horses … he gets on with them all.'

I flopped down, my chin resting on my front paws which were stretched out ahead of me. I noticed that she didn't mention archbishops.

It was one of those drizzly, London afternoons when leaden clouds shroud the skyline, and your every instinct is to curl up on a rug in front of a palace fire and snooze until dinner. We three royal corgis were doing just that in the office of the Queen's ladies-in-waiting. Sophia's desk was unoccupied; she had escorted Her Majesty to a function for Royal Air Force wives in Piccadilly. Tara, meanwhile, was tapping away at her computer, her cool blonde hair, gold earrings and crimson scarf cast in the warm glow of the standard lamp behind her desk.

Midway through the afternoon there was a phone call from downstairs announcing she had a visitor. A short while later one of the palace footmen was ushering a young woman called Justine into the room.

'Thank you so much for making the time to see me.' Justine shook her hand firmly. 'I really feel I could help so many of the others at The Prince's Trust by providing kinesiology.'

'Well, being fairly ignorant on the subject, I think it's a good idea I learn more about it from you first.'

Margaret and I looked up at the visitor. Mid-twenties, her shoulder-length auburn hair like a mane about her shoulders, she looked bright-eyed and enthusiastic while at the same time conveying an air of authority of someone much older than herself.

I remembered an exchange between Tara and Sophia, about how a young girl – made homeless by the death of her mother – had been sponsored through her studies by the Trust several years earlier. Not only had she succeeded beyond everyone's hopes, she had gone on to become something of an ambassador for the Trust, helping others struggling with the same challenges that she had, and using her newly gained knowledge in kinesiology to do so.

The Board of the Trust had been wondering about engaging Justine on a more formal basis, but having had no experience of kinesiology, they thought someone had better find out more; Tara had been asked to do so.

'Can we do this ... over here?' Tara gestured towards where two sofas faced each other across a coffee table next to the window.

Justine nodded.

As the two of them sat down facing each other, I made my way over to welcome Justine and have a good sniff of her ankles. She responded with appreciative patting.

'This is Nelson,' Tara introduced me. 'The newest member of the royal household.'

'So cute!' enthused, Justine. 'Still very young.'

'About eight months,' Tara told her. 'But already making an impression.'

Justine's stockings smelt of many flowers – as though she had been running through a field of fragrant and varied blooms. I didn't think I'd ever encountered such a profusion of scents on any one person's clothing: where had she been?

'Shall I start at the beginning?' enquired Justine.

'Please,' Tara said with a nod.

'Kinesiology is a gentle, but very effective, complementary therapy. Unlike the diagnosis done by a doctor, kinesiology uses muscle monitoring to identify stress patterns in the body.'

'I don't know how much use I'm going to be to you,' Tara told her. 'I'm in very good health.'

'That's fine,' Justine assured her. 'I'll probably confirm that, though kinesiology takes a holistic view, body and mind. Most people come away with some kind of useful insight.'

Tara sat back in her sofa. I could tell she would need some convincing.

'I wonder if you've come across the concept of muscular resistance?'

Then, as Tara shook her head, Justine said, 'It can be a very revealing tool. We may consciously want to achieve something, but if our subconscious mind, our inner programming, is against it, we're really going to struggle. I see this with a lot of the kids through The Prince's Trust. They want to bring about positive changes in their lives. That's what they consciously want. But their best intentions are undermined all the time by the things they believe about themselves, like "I'm not worthy", or "there's no point trying". By identifying these self-sabotaging beliefs, we can get to the root of the problem.'

'Hmm,' said Tara.

'Perhaps I can demonstrate?' offered Justine.

'Of course.'

'If you'd like to put out your arm at shoulder height and resist my pressure to push it down?'

Tara looked surprised by the request, but did as she was asked. Justine didn't seem to be exerting great pressure, but enough for Tara to have to tense her muscles.

'Now, if you'll just say "My name is Tara" while maintaining the same level of pressure.'

Again, Tara did as she was asked, looking somewhat bemused.

'This time,' Justine continued her quietly confident demonstration, 'try "My name is Justine".'

No sooner had Tara uttered the words than her arm slumped downwards.

She glanced at Justine in surprise.

'When you say something that's not in harmony with what you subconsciously believe, muscular resistance is much lower.'

'Heavens!' exclaimed Tara, suddenly engaged. 'Can we try it again?'

Justine resumed her pressure while Tara said "My name is Sophia", her arm collapsing down as quickly as the first time.

'Kinesiology uses this principle, applying it according to five different elements throughout the body.'

'You keep asking questions?'

Justine shook her head. 'All you need to do is lie on the sofa and breathe.'

Moments later, after answering a few questions about her overall state of health, Tara was lying on her back, head resting on the arm of the sofa and focusing on her breath. Justine perched on the coffee table and was pressing on Tara's wrist with one hand, while moving the other, in curious, slow dancing movements, some distance above her body.

I sat at Justine's feet, watched the proceedings intently.

'I'm not picking up any physical issues,' she said.

'Uh-huh.'

'Would you like to see if there's anything on an emotional level that may need attention?'

'Fine.'

The process went on for a while before Justine asked her to focus her gaze to one side, then the other, all the time that she pushed down gently on Tara's wrist. Sometimes, I noticed, it would be less resistant than others, but I had no idea why that would be so. Something to do with the position of her other hand above Tara's body? And was she holding something in it?

After a while, Justine gently pulled back. 'We can probably stop there,' she said.

Tara resumed her previous, sitting position. Apart from touching her wrist, Justine had had nothing else to work with. What information about Tara could she possibly have gleaned?

Justine responded to Tara's look of curiosity with a smile.

'As I said earlier, no physical problems except, perhaps, a little dehydration.'

Tara's expression remained unchanged.

'Emotionally speaking, I did identify a fairly strong sense of rejection.'

'What?' Tara laughed in disbelief.

There was compassion in Justine's eyes as she nodded. 'A feeling of deep loss in a relationship. Something which perhaps has made subsequent relationships difficult? Perhaps made you want to push people away if you fear they may get too close?'

'I can't believe …!' Raising her hands to her face, Tara was suddenly struck by Justine's discovery. 'But that was years ago.'

Justine nodded. 'Ten to fifteen years ago was my guess.'

Tara gazed into the mid-distance. 'Fifteen,' she confirmed. 'And you got all that from …?'

'Our bodies never lie. All the landmarks of our emotional lives – our beliefs – become part of our physical being.'

Tara held her gaze evenly. 'I hardly know what to say.'

'It surprises most people. It came as a big surprise to me when I discovered it. The main thing is to use this in a helpful way. Once we become aware of buried issues, we can deal with them at source.'

'You're saying we can sabotage our own relationships without realizing it?'

'The subconscious mind,' Justine said tactfully, 'is far more powerful than the conscious one. You know the tip of the iceberg image? Most of our behaviour is automatic, operating without the need for conscious thought. When an idea becomes lodged deep down, like the idea that we are unloved, or unlovable, then even if we really want a relationship to work, we will follow the established script, making us act out in ways to fulfil that programming, perhaps by choosing incompatible partners, or behaving destructively when things are going well.'

'My goodness!'

'The important thing is to apply a remedy. To replace the negative programing with positive expectations.'

Tara glanced towards the door of the office, which was ajar.

'I'm sorry,' said Justine.

'No, no.'

'This work takes us straight to the heart of things.'

Tara was shaking her head. 'I would never have even guessed, all these years later …'

Justine nodded. 'Perhaps you can make sense of certain things?'

Tara held her gaze.

'Usually it's what we say or do when we're not being mindful. When we're distracted or stressed out, and, instead of behaving as we'd consciously like to, our subconscious programing shows through.'

'Other people get mixed messages?'

'Exactly,' said Justine with a nod. 'And when our words conflict with our behaviour, it's what we do that other people pay attention to, not what we say.'

This conversation was reminding me of the very similar one I'd overheard, between the Queen and the positive dog trainer. Both dogs and humans, it seemed, shared the same ability to sense when things weren't quite right. Both could detect if what someone was saying was merely an act.

Justine shrugged. 'We're all works in progress. It takes courage to be open about our flaws, but that's what makes us authentic. Winston Churchill's black dog, for instance.'

Over by the fireside, one and a half ears pricked up momentarily.

'Black dog' was not a phrase I'd heard before and it confused me.

There was a long pause as Tara regarded Justine carefully. 'I only wish I knew half of what you do when I was your age.' She smiled.

'Thank you!' Justine glanced down modestly.

'You've given me a lot to think about. And I think your services could be invaluable to many who come into contact with the Trust.'

That night was one of the rare occasions when Her Majesty enjoyed dinner, just for the family, at Buckingham Palace. Winston, Margaret and I were in attendance, lying on the carpet a short distance away from the table, and ever-watchful of our younger family members who may, in a soft-hearted moment, surreptitiously slip us a morsel from the table.

'What was that about Winston Churchill having a black dog?' I quizzed Winston, flopping beside him, and fixing Kate with a look of winsome adoration.

'Not an actual dog,' said Winston. 'Figure of speech, dear boy. It means he suffered from depression.'

'Do black dogs get very depressed?'

'Shouldn't think so.'

I mulled it over. Up until that point I hadn't known that humans might associate the word "dog" with a feeling of unhappiness.

'I suppose we do make humans unhappy sometimes,' I remarked plaintively.

Winston looked over at me, cocking his head. 'You're not still dwelling on the A of C?'

'It's just ...'

'Let go! Move on! Like that woman this afternoon was saying, If you wait till you're perfect before you accept yourself, you never will.'

I leaned over and nuzzled Winston, licking his neck. Sometimes it seemed to me he was the wisest dog in the world.

Whether what happened next was deliberate, I can't say, but the timing seemed significant. Only moments later a cloud of the most noxious stench rose up to engulf everyone in the room.

Charles's reaction was instant. 'Winston!' he spluttered, rising to his feet and flapping his hand across his face to no avail.

'I think we should go next door for a few moments.' Her Majesty rose, leading the way with quiet dignity, while the butler produced a cigar lighter from his pocket and unleashed a gas-consuming flame.

Margaret and I both looked at Winston askance.

'Better out than in,' he explained.

'But really!' Margaret was deeply unimpressed.

'We all have our flaws,' he snorted. 'Embrace them!'

Several months later the Queen paid a visit to the Archbishop of Canterbury at his official residence, Lambeth Palace. It was a Friday afternoon and we were on our way to Windsor. On arrival, Police Detective Lewis took us for a walk in the Archbishop's garden, while the Queen went inside to discuss churchly matters.

It wasn't a lengthy meeting – barely long enough for the royal corgis to leave our collective mark on the most important trees and shrubs. A vibration in Detective Lewis's phone in her pocket summoned us to the side door from which Her Majesty would be leaving the building.

It was a perfectly tranquil day when the ancient, wooden door opened to reveal the Queen and Archbishop in quiet conversation. Looking out, when he saw the corgis, the Archbishop immediately smiled.

'Oh – I'll have to call Mitzy. She *will* be pleased.'

Moments later the two humans and one poodle were emerging, Mitzy skipping over to greet us, barking excitedly and tail wagging frantically. She had exchanged wet-nosed greetings with all three of us before the Queen and Archbishop had caught up with us, the A of C bending to pat us warmly.

It didn't escape me that neither Mitzy, nor the Archbishop, had shown a moment's hesitation in wanting to greet me. Nor was their warmth in any way contrived. It was as if the Highgrove moment had never happened. Or if it was remembered, it seemed of no importance at all.

For a while we dogs were allowed to scamper on the lawn, before the time came to get back in the car. Her Majesty and the Archbishop exchanging waves as our car pulled away.

That day's drive out to Windsor was a time of some reflection. I wondered how it was possible that something of so little importance to others could assume such great significance in one's own mind. How self-doubt could grow so easily if left unchecked. I thought how events in the past could continue to affect us even if we didn't realise it, as had been the case for poor Tara.

But at least there *were* ways to leave the past behind – the advice of the kinesiologist had confirmed that. And, in the meantime, recognising that we all have flaws was a vital part of self-acceptance. Being who we are, without pretence, was vital in allowing us to be authentic.

I remembered Winston's sage advice – *'Let go'* – feeling relief almost palpable as a wave passed through me. And so I did. The only moment that mattered was this one, sitting on the car seat next to the Queen and my fellow corgis on a beautiful Friday afternoon, with England's green and pleasant land sliding by, as lovely as it ever had been.

Later that afternoon, Her Majesty was being consulted on forward planning by her secretary, Julian.

'The Braemar Gathering.' He nodded towards a folder on her lap, containing various paperwork. 'Does that all look in order?'

The Queen glanced down, reading a margin note she'd previously made.

'Ah yes.' She nodded. 'We need to have a word with Huchens.'

Moments later her head of security was in our midst, imposing and formidable.

'Did you have a chance to enquire about that schoolboy?'

'Simpson, ma'am. Who was being bullied by Jenkins?'

'That's the one.'

'I spoke to his mother last week. Jenkins has changed his attitude entirely. He has become Simpson's greatest protector. Mrs Simpson says her son's study is so quiet that you can hear a pin drop.'

'Very good.'

'In fact, some sort of friendship has been struck up between the boys.'

The Queen raised her eyebrows. 'Even better.'

'In that case,' she nodded towards Julian, 'we should invite Jenkins and his band to Braemar.'

'The massed bands, ma'am?' enquired her secretary.

'Yes,' she replied. Before saying uncertainly, after a moment, 'No.'

Then, responding to Julian's enquiring expression, 'I'd like to put him in the spotlight, so to speak, just for a short while.'

Julian pondered for a moment before suggesting, 'You could give him a solo?'

'Splendid.'

'Is there anything in particular you'd like him to play?'

Her Majesty thought about this for a while, frowning in contemplation, before Huchens volunteered, '"A Scottish Soldier"?'

She considered this briefly, before shaking her head.

'"Scotland the Brave",' Julian offered, somewhat obviously.

It was a moment before she looked up first at Julian and then her security chief. 'Under the circumstances, I think it should be "Amazing Grace".'

Six

You may very well be wondering by now if there are any limits to the Queen's patience when it comes to her corgis? Not only did she observe my incontinence without comment. She shrugged off the worst security breach in several years – one caused by my impetuous behaviour – as though it was of little consequence. *And* you will have noticed that not a sharp word was spoken even when I humped the Archbishop of Canterbury's leg.

Is there nothing, you may very well ask, capable of provoking Her Majesty's wrath?

Let me assure you, my fellow subject, that even though the Queen is a model of restraint and forbearance, she is mostly certainly human. Possessing the firm expectation that others will act in accord with their highest purpose, there are certain things guaranteed to incur her disapproval. As I learned the day of the garden party.

There is a decided *frisson* at Buckingham Palace in the lead up to a garden party. Even though the Queen entertains regularly, everything from receiving her prime minister each Wednesday evening, to hosting banquets for visiting heads of state, garden parties have a particular quality to them.

Perhaps it is the outdoor setting, away from the pomp of red carpets, gilded chairs and crystal chandeliers. No doubt it also has to do with the kinds of people who attend – not the rich and titled, but instead a wide cross-section of people from Britain, the Commonwealth, and even further afield. Almost all of them, bitsas.

There is an informality about such events. A spontaneity far removed from the carefully scripted speeches of most public events. For this very reason, those who were comfortable in their own coats – like Winston – welcomed the opportunity to mix and mingle. But those who feared what might happen if members of the public were given free access to palace grounds and certain public rooms – like Margaret – became increasingly anxious.

For weeks leading up to the event she would raise her snout with an air of foreboding, as though, at this very minute, hawk-faced trade union leaders in smoke-filled cellars were plotting their raids on the dessert trolleys. Whenever Julian, Her Majesty's secretary, brought up the subject of the impending garden party at morning briefings, Margaret would lift her head from the Persian rug, lips quivering to reveal her bared teeth.

On one of our daily walks I asked Margaret, perhaps naively, what she had against garden parties. Her expression turned very severe as she spoke of things well beyond my comprehension. Eyes bulging and saliva flecking the sides of her mouth, it was clear that she felt very strongly about the matter. Her diatribe only came to an end when I asked her about a phrase she'd used. It had a pleasant sounding rhyme to it, but I knew from the way she spoke that it was a Very Bad Thing.

'When you say "reds under the beds", who exactly do you mean, Margaret?' I asked.

'The Socialists!' she snarled. 'They want to bring down the monarchy! To drive us out of Buckingham Palace.'

'Why would anyone want to do that?' It was the first time I'd heard of such a notion and it seemed preposterous. For the first time I found myself becoming alarmed.

'Because they are communists! Red!'

'And … and these reds,' I wanted to be clear. 'Is it the flower beds they're under?'

'Oh,' she snapped, tugging her at her lead to get away from me. 'You stupid boy!'

I was quite used to Margaret's displays of ill temper. They always seemed to involve a 'matter of principle'. But they rarely lasted long.

She continued her deep wariness in the days leading up to the garden party. I didn't bring up the subject again with her, for fear of once more exposing my very deep ignorance.

Although I did ask Winston what he thought.

'Margaret says that reds under the beds want to drive us from the palace,' I told him. 'Is it true?'

Winston snorted contemplatively, before saying, 'It is true. But I wouldn't make too much of it, dear boy. They've been saying the same thing for a hundred years and it hasn't happened yet. You know –' he drew himself up, as he always did when about to impart a special piece of wisdom '– a life lived in fear is no life at all.'

But for a single phrase, my fellow subject, the course of that year's garden party may have taken a very different turn – and who knows where things may have ended up? But it was less than half an hour before the Queen made her public appearance that I made my way through her suite. She was in her drawing room with Julian being told about some of the guests who had been invited that day, including a group of Chelsea pensioners. Outside the sun was shining and skies only partly cloudy – a wonderful day for the event.

I knew that Margaret had already taken herself downstairs. Visitors were already trickling in through the gates and she was no doubt scrutinising them rigorously. Winston lay sprawled under an occasional table next to the Queen, snoring softly. Not feeling in the least bit sleepy, and needing to fill in the time until we accompanied Her Majesty downstairs, I found myself idly wandering through the Queen's private suite of rooms. These included a spacious dressing room, never of much interest to a corgi, as well as her bedroom. I was strolling past this too when I glanced through the door.

Which was when I saw the thing: red.

And on her bed.

Its audacious, scarlet plumage a-quiver in the afternoon breeze.

I froze. Paw mid-air, I could hardly believe what I was seeing!

Was this not exactly what Margaret had warned of? And on the very day of the garden party? The brooding menace that threatened to chase us out of our beloved home. No longer was it under the bed – it had already advanced on top of it!

I set off like lightning. Racing to the bed for Queen and country. Leaping onto it. Launching myself at the loathsome fiend and tearing into its bright, red feathers. While initially it remained inert, as soon as I had it in my jaws it responded with a painful sting, a rubber-like cord unravelling round my snout like a tentacle, delivering a sharp, metallic thwang to my nose.

So this was how socialists operated? Well, I would show it!

I wasn't going to be cowed by its stings and arrows. I was in the service of Her Majesty the Queen, my valour needed every bit as much as any knight of the realm. Stout of heart and with implacable resolve I planted both front paws on the threatening beast and tore into it even more vigorously.

Growling and chewing, I was beginning to dominate the wretch, at least it hadn't responded with any further barbed tentacles, when Her Majesty strode into the room.

'Nelson!' she shouted. Not in horror or shared outrage at the threat to our way of life. But in wrath.

I looked up.

'Get down here at once!' She pointed to the floor.

Bewildered, I slunk off the bed and cowered. I had rarely seen her so angry. And never before with me.

Tara appeared in her doorway moments later and looked towards the bed.

'Your hat!' Aghast, the two of them stared at the scattered plumage and torn remnants.

I could hardly believe my ears. Surely that wasn't all it had been? The Queen was looking at a clock. 'It's not the hat itself that concerns me,' said the Queen. 'There are people outside who have been looking forward to this afternoon for months. I don't wish to be late.'

I noticed that Her Majesty was wearing a summery dress with red blossoms, precisely the same shade as the item I had just destroyed. Was I a dog who had mistaken a hat for a socialist?

The Queen and her lady-in-waiting hurried to the dressing room where they sought out first one hat, then another. What Her Majesty wears is always carefully considered, and usually decided well before. Intricate planning goes into her outfit for every event and she has access to unlimited variations of dresses and hats. Getting the right match for each occasion is a task she usually delegates to her dressers, merely confirming their choice, or requesting a change, a day or two in advance, when the items are brought out of storage. But she had already let her dresser go this afternoon. And finding a suitable hat at last minute from the limited number available wasn't easy.

'Plain yellow?' I heard Tara offer a suggestion.

'It's a bit windy today for that one. Last time I wore it, it almost blew off. What do you think of this?'

'Not an ideal match for the red.'

'No.'

The two of them spent time trying out a number of variations – none of them anywhere near the perfect match which I had so misguidedly destroyed.

Then I heard the Queen say, 'Fifteen minutes. I don't want to keep them waiting any longer. I shall simply go hatless.'

'That would be unusual.'

'Indeed.' There was resolve in Her Majesty's voice, along with a strong sense of duty. 'But what of it?'

As the two of them walked from the dressing room and out of the Queen's private rooms she continued, 'It's my own fault. I should have realised it would be a temptation leaving it where I did.'

Winston, roused from his slumbers, was trotting behind the two of them. If he was surprised by Her Majesty's lack of a hat, he didn't mention it. I held back, somewhat, ears drooping. I had never felt so mortified.

We made our way along a corridor to the staircase, and down several flights of steps before reaching the public rooms. About to make our appearance, the Queen turned to the two of us. 'Now, best behaviour, little ones!' she said in a kindly voice. I knew she meant it for me, which made me feel all the more undeserving.

There was a curious atmosphere when we walked onto the lawn. I was by now quite used to royal entrances. As one of Her Majesty's representatives - albeit of the hat-eating kind – I had some experience of how people responded when coming face to face with their monarch.

The mood that afternoon was different. There was a strangely brittle laughter as we first arrived, along with an undercurrent of embarrassment. Huchens, who usually kept within short distance of the Queen but was rarely right beside her, accompanied her the moment she made her entrance. His face seemed even more pink than usual.

After the initial awkwardness, things seemed to settle down. The mere presence of the Queen and other family members prompted an outpouring of warmth and excitement, as well as that powerful sense of benevolent expectation that accompanied her wherever she went. Yes, today was an occasion of celebration and lightness, a rare chance to engage with one of the most famous beings on planet earth. But for many it would also prove to be an unexpected encounter with the Queen's radiant expectations.

As Her Majesty began being introduced to people, we corgis made our own way across the gardens. I noticed that

Margaret was being admired by a group of Chelsea pensioners in their immaculate red uniform. Winston made his way
towards a group of younger people. Within moments, mini-
pizzas were falling to the grass. I followed quickly in his wake,
the two us wolfing down the food appreciatively.

'So, what was that all about upstairs?' he asked, after
we had ensured that not a single crumb of pastry or wisp
of cheese remained on the lawn. We were both feeling more
replete – and conversational.

I told him about the red thing I'd seen on Her Majesty's
bed, its feathers tremulous in the breeze. How it had seemed
to be a sinister presence in light of what Margaret had said
about reds under beds. How I had leapt up and torn it to
shreds in a trice – yes, I did exaggerate a little – before the
Queen had arrived. How she was not amused.

Winston, however, was amused. Greatly. 'Go on!' He
nudged me playfully with his snout. 'You didn't!' In a rare
burst of energy, he ran across the lawn, tumbling in front of
a flower bed, stubby legs poking into the air, snorting and
chortling at what I'd told him.

'You didn't! You didn't!'

'I'm afraid I did, Winston,' I admitted ruefully.

He was doing it again, the mischievous energy of that
afternoon prompting him to make another short burst across
the lawn. Some of Her Majesty's guests were turning to watch,
laughing at our playfulness.

'You didn't! You didn't!'

'But I did!'

Eventually he'd settled down enough to say, 'You didn't
realize that "reds under beds" is just a figure of speech?'

'You're not saying –'

'A turn of phrase? A metaphor?'

I knew about metaphors. 'No, I didn't.' I was defensive. 'How am I supposed to know what a socialist looks like?'

'Well, not like a hat!' Winston was still snuffling with mirth. 'Sorry, Nelson! It's just too funny!'

He regarded my downhearted expression carefully before asking, 'What?'

I had to look away for a moment before replying. 'It's just that you're always talking about the importance of the Golden Rule.'

'As you sow, so shall you reap. Do unto others. Cause and effect. Taught by all the great spiritual leaders.'

'Does it mean I will experience terrible things because I destroyed the Queen's hat?'

'Oh, I see,' replied Winston, before cocking his head. 'Your motivation was to protect and defend, not to destroy. Intention is key. Besides, the Queen has a way of drawing something good even from the bad. Call it alchemy.'

I sighed. 'I just wish that beings would say what they mean sometimes.'

'Ah! Words and the meaning of words. A timeless quest. If you knew the meaning of the phrase "reds under beds" you wouldn't have destroyed the Queen's hat.'

We stood contemplating the truth of this as we surveyed the Buckingham Palace gardens on what was turning out to be a balmy afternoon.

'If only I knew what every word meant,' I mused. 'That would make me the wisest dog in the land.'

'Not the wisest, Nelson. The most knowledgeable, perhaps, but not the wisest.'

I looked at him, enquiringly.

Winston fixed me with an expression of the deepest significance. '*Knowing* the meaning of words is mere knowledge,' he intoned. '*Experiencing* the meaning of words is wisdom.'

Sensing my uncertainty, he continued. 'Wisdom is what happens when our understanding of a thing deepens to the point that it changes our behaviour.'

He raised his snout and parsed the air for a few moments. Take the words "stop and smell the roses".'

I cocked my head. 'A metaphor.'

'What do the words mean?'

Winston *had* gone profound on me. 'Meaning …' I tried to think of an explanation. 'Don't be in so much of a hurry all of the time that you ignore the things that can make you happy.' My stump twitched in anticipation.

'Many beings know what the words mean,' said Winston, implying I had answered him correctly. 'But how many act like they do?'

My immediate thoughts were of the people who constantly streamed through nearby St James's Park, where there were often the most beautiful flourishes of verdant flowers. Many of the commuters were deeply engrossed in important conversations on their mobile phones. Or seemed intent on hurrying to their destination.

From somewhere amongst my earliest memories came an actual bed of roses, gorgeous and perfumed, not far from The Crown, where the Grimsleys had spent so many a Saturday evening. I couldn't remember them stopping once to admire it, or even remarking on the display.

Of course you can never tell what goes through the mind of another being. But if outward behaviour was any clue, I realised, Winston was absolutely right: knowledge was commonplace. Wisdom, on the other hand, was rare.

I looked over at where Margaret was trotting briskly about the legs of the guests Her Majesty was about to meet. I doubted a single mini-pizza had passed her lips this afternoon.

'Sometimes I think you are the wisest dog in the land, Winston' I told him.

'Very good of you to say.' There was genuine warmth in his gravelly voice. 'But you know, wisdom in someone else is only so good as long as that someone else is around. One needs to cultivate it oneself.' Then as he followed my glance. 'And don't be too hard on those who will probably never find it. Most beings are not on the same path as you and me. At least, not in this lifetime.'

I looked over at Winston with profound gratitude. Although his remark was typically mysterious, I knew enough to gather that he was saying we had something in common.

'Does that make us special?' I ventured, hesitantly.

'Indeed, dear boy,' said he.

When the Queen returned indoors at the end of the garden party, she was accompanied not only by we three corgis and the rest of her family, but also by Huchens. The event was deemed a success by Her Majesty and her senior staff, with all comers seeming to enjoy themselves.

But she did have a question. 'Come on, Huchens, out with it,' she demanded, once the two of them had left the public area of the palace and were behind closed doors. 'You've followed me like a shadow all afternoon.'

The puce colour returned to the cheeks of her security chief. 'We had an incident earlier.'

'Nothing serious, obviously?' confirmed Her Majesty.

'It may have been. It revealed a lapse in our defences.'

'What happened, exactly?'

'You don't need to be concerned with the specifics –'

'Huchens!' It was rare for the Queen to be so imperious.

'Very well, ma'am. We had a streaker.'

Her Majesty paused for just a moment. 'Good heavens! At the garden party?'

'Exactly.'

'I hope he didn't upset anyone.'

'None of the guests, so far as I'm aware. But he upset me.' Huchens was stern. 'He … flaunted himself at the exact moment when you were supposed to make your appearance. Had you not been uncharacteristically delayed, it would have been profoundly embarrassing.'

'Well,' said the Queen, 'we have Nelson to thank, then. He took it into his head to dismember my hat. In so doing, it seems that he prevented a more serious calamity.'

'He did.' Huchens glanced at me only to indulge Her Majesty. I had the sense that the former SAS warrior had no truck with happy coincidences, especially those involving destructive corgis.

'Was he good-looking then, this streaker?' asked the Queen.

'I – I – I mean to say, ma'am –'

'Yes?'

There was a pause while he formulated an answer. 'That falls completely outside my area of professional expertise.'

'Oh, don't be an old stick-in-the-mud, Huchens.' The Queen flicked her handbag against the side of her leg. 'One is simply curious.'

'Well, if you really want to know ...'

'I do.'

'He was a thirty-something Caucasian male. Lanky. Tattooed. Needed a decent haircut. And from what I could see *nothing* about him that was unusual or impressive.'

'Oh, good,' said the Queen with just the hint of a mischief. 'We wouldn't want to have missed out on anything ... impressive.'

But it wasn't until the following day that the full impact of my ignorant attack on Her Majesty's hat became clear. Next morning, Lady Tara was browsing through that day's media cuttings, which were always waiting for her by the time that she arrived. Several newspapers had reported on the garden party – large, colour photographs of some of the more interesting or well-dressed guests.

All the royal correspondents noted the fact that the Queen hadn't been wearing a hat. What was the significance of this departure from normal royal protocol, they wondered? Was there a deeper meaning to it? Did it mark a new and refreshing informality? Milliners, hair stylists and non-verbal communications experts had all been canvassed for their views. No mention was made at all of the possibility that one of her corgis had been responsible for savaging the red menace.

By far the most popular photograph of the day showed Her Majesty at the centre of the group of Chelsea pensioners, the blooms of her dress matching their jackets, as they all beamed broadly into the camera.

'She's a saint!' one of the pensioners had decided, after meeting her. It was the phrase that had given the papers their headline for another, entirely unforeseen reason. It just so happened that the photograph had been taken later in the afternoon, but which time the sun had moved westwards. Its lengthening rays, shining directly through the Queen's hat-less hair, producing a halo effect so that the pensioner's words appeared self-evident. 'The Queen's halo', some of the papers referred to it as.

'Wonderful!' exclaimed Tara, leaping from her seat and taking the folder of press cuttings in the direction of Her Majesty's office.

Pausing at the door she glanced over before summoning me. 'Come, Nelson! I am sure the Queen will want to see you. It seems like you have given her the best media day so far this year!'

Across the carpet, Winston regarded me with amusement. As I got up to follow Tara, I walked past him.

'See what you mean about the Queen and alchemy.'

Winston snorted. 'Look sharp,' said he.

Seven

O ne of the highlights of life as a royal corgi happens each Friday morning when we're fed our weekly bone. Each of us in turn is presented with a delicious, meat-encrusted shank. We carry our treasure to a spot in the small staff garden – or if the weather is inclement, a corner of the laundry – where we give free rein to our atavistic urges, gnawing, grinding and chewing for the next hour in a state of contented absorption.

You can tell something about a canine from the way he eats his bone, don't you think? Winston would attack his with gusto, snorting and slavering with wanton abandon. No less eager, Margaret gnawed her bone with diligent rigour, removing every last scrap of meat from one end to the other. Having never seen a bone before joining the royal household, I was initially unsure what to do with it. But within a few minutes I had taken to the delights of shank-chewing, relishing the tasty, marrow-mashing, tooth-sharpening joy of it.

When the bone-chewing came to an end I observed another interesting difference between Winston and Margaret. His jaws tender from all the clenching and tugging, Winston would take his bone to the side of the garden, where small terracotta pots were stacked, and drop it beside them, next to several other bones from Fridays past.

Margaret had a very different notion of bone disposal. Making her way to the flower bed at the back of the garden she'd use both paws and snout to dig a hole deep enough to conceal what remained of her bone, before covering it up with loose soil. She'd emerge from the flower bed, her nose and face unfamiliarly smudged with earth. But she'd have about her an air of quiet accomplishment.

The first time I witnessed this, I felt a curious tug. Some deep-down instinct I had never even known that I possessed seemed to impel me to do just the same thing. Picking up my own bone, I made my way over to the flower bed, placing it at the side.

'We're supposed to bury bones?' I confirmed, as she covered up her own, flicking the soil with all four paws with ease of practice.

'Waste not, want not,' she said.

I couldn't avoid looking over to where Winston was dropping his by the flowerpots, rather casually I thought.

'Why isn't Winston burying his?'

'You'll have to ask him,' she replied.

As it happened, Winston was making his way towards us. 'An ancient canine instinct,' he nodded towards where Margaret was making her way off the flower bed and began wiping her snout on the lawn. 'Preserving food in case of future shortages.'

I registered this with interest. 'Have royal corgis ever gone short?' I asked.

'Never,' he replied emphatically.

'The past does not equal the future,' observed Margaret quietly. While she didn't hesitate to disagree with Winston from time to time, she would always do so with a genuine regard for his elder corgi status.

'True,' he agreed with equanimity.

Wondering what to do with the bone between my front paws, I asked Winston, 'You don't think there will be … shortages?'

He cocked his head. 'I don't,' he said, 'but that's not why I leave my bones above ground.'

I could tell he was in one of his enigmatic moods, as what he said next confirmed.

'There are many ways to hide a thing. Concealing it underground is one way. Another is to hide it in plain sight.'

'But …' I struggled to understand him '… if something is in plain sight, doesn't that mean it's not hidden?'

Margaret was pretending to be deeply absorbed in removing loose soil from her snout with her front paw.

Winston fixed me with a knowing expression. 'That is what common sense might tell you, dear boy,' he said. 'But not all sense is common. Look sharp.'

I had ended up leaving my bone behind the low, outdoor shed housing the rubbish bins, an action which became engrained as habit over time. But every Friday when we sat with our bones I would also gnaw over Winston's words about things being hidden in plain sight. What could he possibly mean?

I began to discover the answer to this quite some months later, and regrettably Winston wasn't present at the time. It was during the deepest of wintry days in January, with the outside world a place of unremitting bleakness, the branches of the trees outside Windsor Castle stark and barren, and the grey skies leaden with rain. The Queen was just emerging from a very bad cold, and it seemed that poor Winston had also succumbed to a seasonal bug, eating less food than usual, and with none of his customary zeal. He had taken to spending a great deal of time in his basket.

All three of us were with Her Majesty in her private sitting room one afternoon when, having glanced at a clock, she rose from her chair and made her way towards the door. Winston remained in his basket, his breathing laboured. Margaret looked up, ears alert. She was usually punctilious about accompanying Her Majesty on even the most routine of encounters, but that afternoon she seemed not to realize that the Queen was on her way to a meeting.

I followed Her Majesty as she left the sitting room. Her movements were slow but deliberate on account of her still somewhat frail state. She took her time slipping into her coat and making her way from her private quarters. I had no idea where she was going, but I did have an idea who she was planning to meet.

As I trotted along beside her, aware of my responsibilities as the only royal corgi on duty that afternoon, I knew that during her most recent appointments meeting with private secretary, Julian, no mention had been made of an engagement today.

'Does the Queen ever receive unscheduled visitors?' I remembered Winston asking me during those early months, before answering his own question emphatically, 'Never! Nobody just drops in to see Her Majesty. Nobody, that is, except for Michael.'

The Queen's footsteps led her through the castle and, shadowed discreetly by security, in the direction of St George's Chapel.

For me, St George's Chapel is the most magical chamber in the whole castle. It was in this sacred place that members of the royal family had been married over the centuries. Here too that the remains of kings and queens of Britain have been interred for the past six hundred years, including that of the first Queen Elizabeth in 1492.

In the semi-darkness, with the only light coming from the lamps in the warm, wooden choir stalls, and the gold of the altar, there was a sense of mysticism, of connection to other dimensions of experience as Her Majesty and I made our way to the front of the chapel, along the black and white chequered floor. Above us, rows of heraldic flags were draped from both sides of the chapel, standards of ages past, their magnificent colours rich with symbolism.

As security remained discreetly at the door, the Queen went to sit on one of the choir stalls nearest the altar. Her movements fragile, she sat down carefully, contemplating the altar, before taking in much more than only that. It was as though ancient mystery reverberated down the ages to this particular place, on this silent, mid-winter afternoon. Had the energy of extraordinary events and people become imbued in the fabric of this medieval building? Was the Queen able to slip into an experience of timelessness which enabled her to put whatever was happening in her life into different perspective? I wondered if Her Majesty visited here to be touched by the transcendent, to experience a special kind of peace.

For a while she remained in silent contemplation. Then there came a noise from the entrance to the chapel and we looked up to see Michael approaching. In a white cloak that seemed more monk's robe than raincoat, he seemed to reflect the warm, gold of the altar as he came closer, his bright blue eyes dazzling in the pale light.

As he drew closer he paused, bowing. 'Your Majesty,' he said, greeting her.

She met his eyes with a grateful smile. 'I'm pleased to see you,' she said. 'Very nice cloak.'

'The colour of the moon,' he responded. 'In Christian mysticism, Jesus can be seen in a robe of this colour. It symbolises resurrection.'

He stepped over where I'd settled at her feet, before sitting on the pew beside her. Gazing in the same direction as her, after a while he observed in a soft voice, 'In all the world, there are few places of such antiquity and transcendence. You can feel the devotional energy like milk and honey.'

She nodded. 'The cross is always a source of deep contemplation about what it means to be human.'

'Indeed, ma'am. A universal symbol. The horizontal line representing matter. The vertical representing spirit. Man as the intersection of spirit and matter.'

'Many people today think of themselves as nothing more than matter.'

Michael nodded. 'It's unfortunate how many have been so seduced by conventional appearances they will even deny the possibility of anything beyond their limited senses. But perception is misleading. The material world is not as it seems. Little do many people understand that the matter they believe to be so solid is nothing other than their own imagining.'

The Queen shifted in her seat. 'Even when one knows this to be true, one still needs to deal with … conventional concerns,' she observed.

'Of course. The dilemma. But in doing so, we need to recollect that what we are witnessing is merely the dance of appearances, whose only importance is the opportunity it gives us to act in accordance with the divine purpose. To manifest God's love.'

Her Majesty sat in silence for a long while considering this, before she observed, 'I suppose I come to this place to be reminded of what you say. Understanding the concepts may be helpful, but it needs to go deeper, doesn't it? We need to truly realize it.'

'Indeed, Your Majesty. Knowledge, on its own, gets us only so far. To be of real benefit, knowledge needs to change our behaviour.'

Although I was resting at Her Majesty's feet, I was paying close attention to every word that was being spoken. Recognising how very similar it was to what Winston had told me at the summer party.

'Contemplation can help. Casting a stone into a tranquil lake has a much greater impact than throwing the same stone into a turbulent sea. So, too, the understanding of a settled mind.'

After a while the Queen turned to Michael. 'I am fortunate to have you to advise me.' Her voice was warm with appreciation. 'Both fortunate and very grateful. It seems to me that we are all surrounded by symbols and wisdom which can be transforming. But we need to learn their meaning.'

'Hidden in plain sight,' agreed Michael.

As he did, I shifted where I was lying on the floor, turned to look at him and pricked up one and a half ears. Again, the exact words Winston had used when stacking his bones beside the flowerpots? Could it be that he had learned his wisdom sitting at Michael's feet?

'Someone seems very interested in what you just said,' observed the Queen.

'Oh, he has been listening to it all very carefully,' said Michael with complete confidence.

I wondered how he could be so sure.

Leaning over to pat me, he asked Her Majesty, 'How is our little alchemist?'

'Coming on in leaps and bounds,' she said with a chuckle. 'Turning base metal into the finest gold.'

'I had no doubt that would happen.'

Her Majesty recounted the recent visit to Gloucester and the rescue of Cara which had led to my being named Nelson.

Michael regarded me closely, warm appreciation showing in his blue eyes.

'A telling start to what will be a most auspicious life.' His words seemed filled with significance.

The Queen regarded him closely. 'I'm so pleased you said that.'

'Without question.' He nodded. 'I see great things ahead for Nelson. Great purpose.'

Great things were not to unfold that same afternoon, however. On leaving the chapel, Her Majesty decided to take a short stroll near the river. I was more than pleased to join her. With security lurking in the background, we set off on that dullest of afternoons, the pallid winter sunlight unable to break through the heavy clouds, the grey riverbanks and spindly silhouettes of branches as dark as before. But after our time in the chapel, the outside world didn't seem so gloomy. As Michael had explained, the way that outward things appeared had to do with the way we saw them. And as beings whose true purpose was the manifestation of love, even a solemn, winter's afternoon could be an invigorating place for adventure.

Without a lead, and Her Majesty making no attempt to keep me by her side, I was soon scampering through the gardens and sniffing curiously in shrubs, pausing to detect what canines or other creatures may have passed this way, and lifting my leg to mark my royal canine territory.

Absorbed in this important activity, I didn't realise how far ahead of me the Queen had progressed until, looking up, I saw her on the path which, inexplicably, angled sharply away from the river bank, before turning back towards it. An unnecessary detour it seemed to me. Seeking to catch up with Her Majesty, I set off at some speed, opting for the short cut.

The earth was dark and wet, I discovered. Muddy.

Very muddy.

Not like any ground I'd ever walked on.

Suddenly I wasn't moving very fast. In fact I wasn't moving at all. I was stuck. My paws were disappearing below the surface. I was sinking into the mud. A putrid swamp at that!

I yelped. Twice. But there was no one to hear me. The path ahead disappeared behind a boathouse and Her Majesty had disappeared with it.

Would a burst of energy be enough to pull me from the mire?

I tried exactly this, only the faster I moved, the more I seemed to get bogged down.

It wasn't just my feet which were below the surface now. I was sinking to my knees! It was becoming a real struggle to stay upright. The greater my efforts to break free, the more I was drawn downwards into the thick, black stench.

As my stomach began to submerge, I became desperate. I barked with all the loud urgency I was able, fixing my attention on where the path emerged from behind the boatshed. A strong gust of wind blowing in the wrong direction meant that the Queen couldn't hear me. But I redoubled my efforts when I saw her making her way from the other side of the boatshed.

She stopped to pause, looked to each side, before glancing behind.

Whether it was my frantic yapping coinciding with a momentary calming of the wind, or Her Majesty detecting a movement in the swamp, I can't say. But she was suddenly turning and returning at speed, then pointing towards me as two dark-clad men from security materialised.

One of these, appearing from behind her, headed first towards the boatshed. Then he was hurrying in my direction, a canoe paddle in his hand. Like all the security men he was large, fast and muscular. In moments he was on the pathway next to me, slipping the oar into the mud underneath my stomach. Using the paddle as a lever he was hauling me upwards. Then he was dragging me towards him.

The Queen, flanked by another security man, was fast approaching as I was safely brought back to the path. There I rewarded my rescuer by shaking myself vigorously, casting a hundred flecks of stinking black mud all over his navy police uniform, not to mention a generous quantity onto his face too.

'Oh, dear!' said the Queen, arriving just in time to see him wipe his face with the back of his hand and succeeding only in smudging the mud more evenly across his features.

'But thank you.' She nodded in my direction. 'We're very grateful.'

Disaster averted, I looked up at her, wagging my now very blackened stump.

'Would you like me to carry him back?' offered security.

'I think he can manage,' replied Her Majesty. 'You're alright, aren't you, Nelson?' She beckoned me.

I took a few muddy steps in her direction.

'But he'll need a bath once we get home.'

Far from recoiling from this prospect, the policeman had obviously been touched by the Queen's unfailing ability to conjure up the highest motives in those around her.

'Very good, ma'am' he replied, as though he could think of no happier way to spend a winter's afternoon than bathing a filthy and foul-smelling corgi.

Soon afterwards, we were making our way back to the castle, this time with me walking most obediently to heel, and the security officer, making no pretence to remain invisible, a short distance behind us.

'So, Nelson, what have we learned from that?' asked Her Majesty conversationally.

To avoid the black swamp, I would have replied. Not to be fooled into taking short cuts across that particular part of the riverbank.

'It was just as Michael said, don't you think?' she continued.

Her Majesty was making a connection that I had so far failed to grasp.

'Perception is misleading,' she reminded me now. 'The material world is not as it seems. Things we believe to be solid can be nothing more than our own imagination.'

I could see what she was getting at, and looked up at her, black booted and chested, no doubt, but my brown eyes bright with appreciation. Far from blaming me for my foolishness, she seemed to be saying that what had happened to me was simply part of being alive.

'The dance of appearances,' she confirmed, a short while later. 'Queens and canines. We can all be fooled.'

Her Majesty is well known for the very wide variety of people she meets at public events such as state banquets, garden parties, Royal Variety concerts, and the numberless other events which crowd her calendar. But as you will already have gathered, my fellow subject, the really interesting meetings, the conversations when intriguing things are said, are almost always held in private.

One such conversation occurred only a few days after our visit to the chapel, and it was the timing of it, as much as the insights themselves, which held a curious synchronicity.

A number of very eminent scientists had joined Her Majesty one afternoon for tea at Windsor Castle for a regular, if not frequent, get-together to explain recent developments in their fields. Seated on a variety of sofas and chairs, the scientists told the Queen and her advisers about important trends to do with the environment, nanotechnology, and alternative energy sources. Lying on one of the rugs, I was much more interested in the mouth-watering display of savoury snacks laid out for afternoon tea.

After the briefing and the discussion that followed, the more interesting part of the proceedings commenced. The Queen and her guests rose to stretch their legs, while a butler and footmen began to serve the refreshments. Winston, Margaret and I did our bit to mix and mingle, and engage in our perennial quest for titbits. Winston, still ailing somewhat from his winter bug, had recovered sufficiently to fix his attentions on a professor who was so genuinely absent-minded that he had, during a previous visit, put a plate of salmon crudités on the floor in order to draw a diagram on his napkin to demonstrate some arcane principle of dematerialisation. Winston had seen to it that the crudités were soon no longer on the plate, thus providing a less arcane manifestation of the same principle.

Margaret was following a very portly environmentalist, perhaps in the hope that his passionate concern for the natural world would extend to herself.

I tried my luck with an artificial-intelligence expert from Cambridge, who was deeply engrossed in conversation with a nanotechnologist. But after a while I realised the two men were so engrossed in their highbrow conversation they hadn't even noticed me.

Which was how I found myself heading back towards where Her Majesty was standing in discussion with a man with a very red nose, and whose field of specialism I couldn't remember, together with a female quantum scientist.

'Most people are still stuck in direct perception theory,' the man was saying. 'They believe that their brains are passive receivers of whatever streams through their eyes, ears and so on. Neuroscientists abandoned that view years ago.'

'Really?' asked Her Majesty. 'Why is that?'

'Apart from anything else, only twenty per cent of fibres in the part of the brain that deals with visual imagery comes from the retina. The other eighty per cent comes from the cortex, which is the part of the brain governing functions like memory.' The neuroscientist had the

Queen's undivided attention. 'So the process of perceiving something is more complex than what people may assume. When we see, or smell or taste something it has far less to do with the thing itself than with our own cognitive processing, especially memory.'

At this point, the female quantum physicist became so excited that she launched into the conversation. A striking woman in her forties, with shoulder-length dark hair, dusky skin and an aquiline nose, her dark eyes were ablaze and her teacup rattled in its saucer.

'What you're saying, Professor Monday, is that what we see is not so much what's out there as what we expect to see?' she asked.

'Precisely!' he chimed. 'We call them "brain-hypotheses".'

'One's experience,' observed the Queen, 'is indirectly related to the external world.'

'Indeed!' His nose deepened its glow. 'What we're doing, at any one time, is projecting brain-hypotheses onto the physical world. We think we're just seeing what's there. But what's there is more a product of our mind than anything.'

'A product of our mind?' asked Her Majesty perceptively. 'Or of our brain?'

'My mistake, Your Majesty.' At this point, Professor Monday's nose turned positively beetroot in colour. 'As a neuroscientist I am unqualified to talk about anything except the workings of the brain. Mind is a different phenomenon.'

'And the two interrelate how?'

'The brain is like a television set. We're learning more and more about how it operates. But we're still unable to explain basic facts like how consciousness is produced. There is a growing conviction that the brain is to consciousness as the

TV receiver is to a broadcast. Even if the TV set breaks down, that is not necessarily the end of the broadcast.'

'And we are creating our own broadcast?' asked the quantum scientist.

'In a manner of speaking,' agreed Professor Monday.

'You see, this goes to the heart of quantum theory too.'

'It does?' Her Majesty was following the exchange with interest.

'Ah!' exclaimed the professor. 'Dr Johar is getting at the non-duality of the observer and the observed.'

His fellow scientist nodded, brushing her hair back from her face. 'Quantum theory tells us that it is meaningless to divide the observing apparatus from the observed.'

The Queen absorbed this with a pensive expression.

I noticed Dr Johar flash an apprehensive glance at Professor Monday, as though she may have waded too far into quantum soup.

Then Her Majesty said, 'Someone was explaining to me only recently how things are much less solid than we believe. How perception is misleading.'

Dr Johar smiled with some relief. 'A quantum scientist, perhaps?'

The Queen regarded her kindly. 'Actually someone from a spiritual background.'

'There is a convergence going on,' said the Professor.

'Is there?'

'Oh, yes!' chimed Dr Johar. 'The esoteric traditions of both the east and the west tell us that we create our own reality, even if we don't recognise this. In my own field, Erwin Schrodinger once said that "Every man's world picture is and always remains a construct of his mind and cannot be proved to have any other existence". There is –' she slid the fingers of both hands together '– a harmony between science and spirituality at their highest levels.'

The Queen nodded. 'If only these essential truths were better understood by all.'

'Quite so, ma'am,' responded the Professor in agreement.

Her Majesty's canine representatives made their way home from this meeting separately. Because I was at the Queen's ankles when she was ushered out of the room to prepare for her next engagement, I went with her. Winston and Margaret would return to our quarters in company of Lady Tara.

Which was why, of all the royal corgis, I alone had the privilege of being with Her Majesty when we both had one of the most extraordinary encounters of our lives.

Dusk was falling as we made our way through the winding corridors of Windsor. There was also an unusual coolness in the air, even though the central heating was usually reliable. Security kept a discreet distance, out of sight both in front and behind, so that it felt as though the two of us were alone as we returned to Her Majesty's private suite.

It so happened that our route passed the entrance to the royal library, a sumptuous room with red, leather sofas, reading lights, and wooden bookshelves that reached all the way to a toweringly high and ornate ceiling. Every one of the shelves was packed with leather-bound volumes, some of which seemed to be of very great antiquity.

The door was ajar and, the room being unused, no lamps had been switched on. But as the two of us passed by, we heard the unmistakeable sound of clicking heels on its wooden flooring.

The Queen paused.

I did too.

Was a family member visiting to find something to read? But if so, who? The footsteps were decidedly female. Her Majesty decided to investigate. Pushing the door wider, she stepped inside. I followed, snout to ankle, as curious as she – if not more so.

We found ourselves looking at a woman who was standing at the window, wearing a black dress and shawl, whom I sensed was, indeed, a family member. But not one I had yet encountered. Nor, to judge by the Queen's expression, had she.

The woman was only a short distance away from us, in silhouette. She was staring outside as though absorbed in a very different time and place. Without the need for words, or even gestures, she conveyed the unmistakeable presence of greatness.

'How do you do?' the Queen greeted her, as she did people of all rank.

At the window, the visitor nodded in acknowledgement, just the once, and very slowly, as though in some form of trance state.

After a while, when it was evident the lady in black wasn't going to say anything further, the Queen asked her directly the question to which we both wanted to know the answer, 'Who are you?'

She turned to look at us directly. Her features were pale, eyes perceptive, and her auburn hair unadorned. And yet, in the instant that she faced us, we were suddenly presented with an altogether different image of bejewelled magnificence,

crown and ermine, sceptre and sword, of a high, white collar
and ancient splendour.

'Elizabeth,' she spoke with absolute clarity.

'And ... why are you here?' Her Majesty was not only
able to maintain her composure. She asked the question with
a tone of kind enquiry, even sympathy for a being who was
somehow lost.

Elizabeth turned back to the window. 'Because ...' she
seemed to be reflecting carefully on her answer '... I am married to England.'

Both Her Majesty and I were following her every movement closely when there was a sound in the passage outside.
A gentle knock at the door.

'Everything alright, ma'am?' came an enquiry from
security.

In an instant, Elizabeth had vanished.

'Quite,' replied the Queen looking down at me. I knew
she was wondering if I had seen Elizabeth too. I pressed my
nose against her ankle wishing to convey that I had been
with her through it all. I had witnessed not just one Queen
Elizabeth, but two, in the same room and in conversation
with each other even though they lived centuries apart.

How many corgis ever got to see that?!

I couldn't wait to tell Winston, but I had to pick my timing carefully. It was dinner time when I got back, and nothing, not even wondrous tales of the supernatural, could be
allowed to distract a dog from his evening meal. It was true
that Winston approached his food with less gusto than usual,
on account of the flu. But all three of us were focused with

single-minded attention on our plates, before we were taken for our post-prandial perambulation by security.

That evening, the three of us kept close together as we walked through the gardens. I knew better than to say anything in front of Margaret. She was not what Winston would call 'sympatico' with any reports of experiences which didn't conform to her own, narrow expectations. And not believing is not seeing.

So it was only much later, when we had retired to our baskets in front of the staff quarters fire, that the opportunity presented itself.

I waited to hear the sound of contented dozing arise from Margaret's basket, before I climbed out of my own and into Winston's. His own snoring was more laboured than usual – but it came to a halt the moment I got onto the blanket beside him.

The words came tumbling out. 'On our way back this evening the Queen and I were in the library and saw this amazing thing. I mean person. I mean, kind of like a person only she wasn't.'

Winston's eyes blinked blearily open. 'Go on.'

'She was Queen Elizabeth. Only the first one. Wearing a black dress. She was there one moment and gone the next.'

'Indeed?' Although surprised, Winston wasn't reacting with quite the degree of excitement I had hoped.

'Did she speak?'

'Only to say –'

'Don't tell me,' he interjected. 'That she was married to England?'

It was my turn for astonishment. 'You've seen her too?'

'Never! What you witnessed today was rare indeed. But not without precedent. The Queen's father also once saw her ghost. She was dressed in black and said she was married to England.'

'So she *was* a ghost?'

I knew nothing about ghosts, but thought they were supposed to be scary. Although the first Queen Elizabeth had possessed a decidedly other-worldly quality, I hadn't found her scary. If anything, I had been struck by a poignant sadness.

'Ghost. Spirit. What do these words actually mean? There is plenty of ... activity at Windsor Castle. As the longest occupied royal castle in Europe, with so many kings and queens of the past thousand years living, dying and buried here, it's hardly surprising. I think of what you witnessed today along the lines of trapped energy.'

I cocked my head to one side.

'Like trapped wind: never comfortable for those involved, and always a relief when it passes.'

'Better out than in?' I confirmed.

'Winston's First Dictum,' he agreed.

I returned to my own basket, lest this unexpected turn in conversation started having a suggestive effect.

It was some minutes later, and I was beginning to doze off, when Winston murmured from his basket, 'Very auspicious that you saw the great Tudor Queen today.'

'Hmm,' I agreed, sleepily.

'A sign, dear boy, that you are ready to take over.'

'Take over what?' I asked drowsily and without much comprehension.

But Winston said nothing more, his cryptic words left to wash beneath the rolling waves of drowsiness as I fell asleep.

One morning soon afterwards, on our return from a stay at Buckingham Palace, we emerged into the staff garden at Windsor to find everything had changed. The walls had been freshly painted. A new outdoor furniture setting took pride of place. And the flower beds were planted in shrubs and a dazzling array of bright, spring flowers – daffodils and crocuses forming a blaze of colour.

Winston stood pensively, observing this announcement of a new season. I romped around the circuit of flowers, taking in the scents and shapes and colours. Margaret proceeded directly to the place in the flower beds where she used to bury her bones. The earth was freshly dug and loose – in itself not a promising development. Making fast progress, she scooped below the surface first in one place then another before turning with a mournful expression and nose covered in potting mix. 'Gone! All of them. They've taken the lot!'

I set off immediately for the outdoor shed housing the garbage bins. The whole area had been cleaned up including, I soon discovered, my own small collection of bones, nowhere to be seen.

Returning to the others I followed where both Margaret and Winston were looking towards the flowerpots, where Winston so casually cast off his own chewed remains. They were still there, only neatly stacked in a pile.

'You like the new garden, corgis?' asked security stepping outside and nursing a mug of coffee in his hand. Then as he noticed where we were looking. 'Don't worry; we didn't throw out all your bones. We wouldn't do that to Her Majesty's canine representatives. We only got rid of the ones that were cluttering up the garden beds and so forth.'

Margaret and I both turned to look at Winston – who tossed his head with a snort.

'Hidden in plain sight,' said he.

Eight

There had been signs – not that we had noticed them. Coughing spells that lasted longer than they should have. Too many meals not fully eaten. Walks when he remained at home saying he just wasn't feeling up to it today. We had thought he was simply having a hard time shaking off the remains of the flu bug he had picked up over winter. With the benefit of hindsight, we should have worked it out sooner. For the simple fact, my fellow subject, was that Winston was gravely ill.

He did try to warn us. But as usual, there was an elusive quality to what he said, so that I didn't hear what he was trying to tell us. In my own case, that was probably because I didn't want to listen.

I remember padding over the lawns to the river near Windsor Castle, our progress slower than in the past, when Winston paused near an extravagant spray of crocuses. 'A spring morning has never seemed so filled with promise as it is today,' he intoned, his voice tremulous.

I raised my nose and inhaled the sweet fragrance of the meadows. To me, the morning seemed exactly like the day before. And how it would no doubt seem tomorrow. And the day after that.

'It is nice,' I agreed. But I did wonder why he was making such a big deal of it.

Dozing by the fire a few evenings later, he rolled over towards me from where he had been stretched out to absorb the full warmth of the fire on his tummy.

'Delightfully toasty!' he enthused, stretching out his legs.

'Hmm,' I agreed, sleepily.

'Nothing nicer than roasting oneself before the hearth!' he continued, as if the experience had led to some kind of epiphany.

I blinked open an eye – the one that wasn't concealed beneath my floppy ear. 'You seem very ...' I searched for the word.

'Very what?'

'Very .... happy with little things. Like a spring morning. Being by the fire.'

'Appreciation.'

'Hmm.'

'And that's because the little things *are* the big things when you don't know how many of them you have left.'

'But doesn't spring come every year?' I asked, combining naivety with thoughtless ingratitude. 'Don't we have a fire every night?'

'That may be,' he replied, without a trace of judgement. 'But do any of us know for sure that we will be around to run through the fields next spring? Or even to sprawl in front of the fire tomorrow night? Life is impermanent, dear boy. Fleeting. None of us knows just how precious it is, until we realise that it will come to an end. Perhaps sooner than we imagine.'

I understood the point that Winston was making. But so gentle was his hinting that I didn't understand why. A more

mature dog would no doubt have worked it out pretty quickly. But I was neither very mature, nor the most observant of
corgis.

I did notice when the subject came up several days later
– and from one of my favourites in the extended household. Harry, along with William and Kate, had set up the
Royal Foundation, a charity working in the areas of special interest to them. It so happened that Harry had invited a small group of former servicemen to Buckingham
Palace. Margaret and I escorted the party – Winston was
feeling poorly – as the young prince showed them around
the palace, including through a number of rooms that most
members of the public would never get to see. Each of the
servicemen had, at some time in the past, been seriously
wounded, and their lives had changed shape as a result of
their wounds. Today's visit was both a celebration of their
survival, and also of the way that several of them had discovered new energy and fresh purpose.

There was Jeff, the former SAS captain now wheelchair-
bound, who had taken up basketball as part of his rehabil-
itation program. He had fast developed such an ability for
the sport that he had excelled himself at the Invictus Games,
before going on to set up innovative training programmes
for paraplegic athletes throughout the country. In recent
months, he had been invited to help train teams in the USA
and Europe.

Leighton was a very different character. The quiet, older
man had been so shattered after imprisonment and torture
in Afghanistan that he had been unable to speak for several months after coming home. Finding his way to a farm
in Cornwall, where he didn't have to interact with anyone

except for his immediate family, after discovering a few unused beehives in the garden shed, he had taken up bee keeping as a hobby. He had found unexpected solace spending time in silent communion with his hives of bees. The hobby had evolved as he discovered he had a particular way with the insects, and he was able to harvest honey made from specific plants. In time, his hand-made, single-origin, organic honey, had come to the attention of one of Britain's most famous chefs – at which point both he, and his bees, were suddenly in demand.

It was intriguing listening to former veterans tell their stories. As so often in the past, I felt how Buckingham Palace was the energetic heart of the nation, sending out waves of inspiration and gathering them back again through stories such as these. That quiet but ever-present rhythm of benevolent purpose, embodied by the Queen herself, coursed through unseen channels and out into the broader world. In the telling of stories such as these, both the people involved, and the inspiration they shared, seemed to return home.

But it was while sharing coffee in the garden afterwards that I overheard a bit of conversation between Harry and one of his guests which struck me most of all.

'Coming to these sorts of events always makes me feel like a fraud,' the former serviceman was saying as I padded up to them. 'Physically and mentally, I have completely recovered. There is absolutely nothing wrong with me.'

Harry was nodding.

'I've got some qualifications. I could study for others. I'm willing to try new things. The problem,' he confessed unhappily, 'is that I just don't know what to do. I actually feel quite envious of people who have a particular talent. A burning passion to build a business, or to become a trainer.' He shrugged. 'Or make honey.'

'I get it,' said Harry.

'I wish I could somehow narrow the range. Work out which of the twenty-five things I could do would give me a sense of purpose.'

Harry paused to reflect for a while before he asked, 'Have you heard about the three questions which can help us work out what really matters to us?'

The former serviceman looked at Harry with interest. 'No, sir.'

'They can be quite useful. Not immediately, always, but after giving them some thought. The first question is: if you knew for sure that you were going to die in exactly 10 years' time, how would you choose to spend your time?'

The serviceman raised his eyebrows – the question evidently being unexpected.

'The second question is: if you knew for sure that you were going to die in exactly one year, how would you choose to spend your time?'

Harry's guest nodded.

'And the third question,' the Prince told him. 'If you were to die in twenty-four hours, what would you have missed?'

'Ah!' The other smiled. Then after a pause, 'Challenging.'

'Exactly,' confirmed Harry.

'If you think you have all the time in the world, what you do next doesn't really matter. I suppose these questions make you face the reality that life is finite.'

I pricked up my one and a half ears. The conversation seemed to mirror what Winston had been saying only a few days ago about the truth of impermanence. Except that Harry's guest had been more direct: life is finite.

I thought of Winston, snorting and wheezing in his basket, unable to sleep. The missed opportunities to mix and mingle, such as this one.

It was only then, my fellow subject, that the penny began to drop.

Dr Axel Munthe had visited Winston several times already. There had been talk of canine influenza and its wide variety of symptoms. Of secondary, respiratory infections and the role of antibiotics. Winston had already had a blood test, but the results had been inconclusive.

As he became suddenly weaker, going off his food almost entirely, Her Majesty consulted Dr Munthe once again. This time, poor Winston had to go into the clinic overnight for further blood tests as well as an X-ray.

When Dr Munthe reappeared, his news was not reassuring. Once again, he had to tell the Queen that the tests hadn't ruled out one thing or another. For the first time he mentioned that there was a chance of something 'sinister' pointing to Winston's advanced age. He was in no position to confirm this. Further diagnostic tests were possible, including an MRI scan. And the very best way of finding out why he wasn't eating, he said, would be to open him up and see exactly what was going on inside his digestive system. But given his weakened condition, it would take him a long time to recover from such invasive action. And besides, he said, if they were to find the worst, there wasn't much they could do with that information. He feared the ultimate prognosis would be the same.

While most of this medical talk was incomprehensible to we dogs, tone of voice and body language was all that we needed. Dr Munthe clearly had no idea what was wrong with Winston. And although he was no pessimist, in his own, measured way he was telling the Queen to prepare herself for the worst.

It was the evening of Dr Munthe's visit that we had retired to the private sitting room at Windsor where the Queen and Philip sat playing Scrabble. A fire glowed in the hearth and we three corgis were scattered about it, dozing contentedly. At one point I looked up, and found Winston's gaze fixed on me. He motioned for me to join him.

As I made my way over and lay down beside him, I couldn't ignore how laboured his breathing had become – even more so than in the past few weeks. It was with some effort that he propped himself up in his basket to face me.

'Nelson.' He looked me straight in the eye. 'I am dying.'

I was startled. 'Don't be silly, Winston. That must be the painkillers talking.'

Dr Munthe had administered a dose which he said would help Winston cope with the attacks of coughing.

'I can feel it in my bones.'

I knew better than to contradict Winston when it came to the subject of his intuition. And because he had rarely been so direct with me, I knew I had to take him seriously.

'But you *can't* die!' I said, feeling helpless.

'Oh, it's the most natural thing in the world,' he said. 'Every one of us must die and if you live well, you have nothing to fear.' From the way he spoke, it was evident that Winston had no concerns about what he faced. 'Death is simply the transition to adventures new.'

There was the longest silence, interspersed only by the occasional crack of a burning log in the fire. Eventually I told him exactly how I felt. 'But I don't want to lose you!' I said, with feeling.

'Sweet of you to say, dear boy,' he replied in a kindly tone. 'But parting is inevitable. We come into the world not knowing anyone. And when we leave, it is on our own too. We separate from everyone who has ever been important to us. From every one of our possessions.'

My mind went to the pile of bones stacked near the flowerpots which Winston had been wise to keep hidden in plain sight.

'It's the same for us all. On the day she dies, even the Queen herself will leave this life with as much as you or me or a beggar in the street.'

I considered this bleak prospect for a moment before I asked, 'Doesn't that make our whole life a bit pointless?'

'Not at all.' He has to pause to take in a few, very laboured breaths before he said, 'It only focuses the mind on what we do take with us.'

I cocked my head, staring at him intently.

'Consciousness,' he spluttered. 'That's what continues. We should take every opportunity we have in this life to make sure that it continues in a positive way.'

'How do you do that?' Winston was revealing a subject I had never thought much about – but which was assuming a sudden, very great importance.

'By creating the true causes of a happy mind.'

I listened to this with interest.

'Can anger lead to contentment?' he asked.

'I … I don't think so.' I didn't want to disappoint him with my answer.

'Never,' he confirmed, his voice weaker than in the past, but still defiant. 'Nor can jealousy lead to peacefulness? Or self-pity to joy? Our main purpose in life is to develop the positive causes of positive mental effects. This is the best way to be happy, not only now, but in the future, when this life ends.'

As so often before, I was struck by Winston's very great wisdom. How he knew the answers to questions I hadn't yet even thought of. But as I mulled over his words, something troubled me. I found myself turning my nose away from him.

'What is it, dear boy?'

'It's ... I don't suppose it's ... anything much.'

'No time to lose,' he managed, before succumbing to a violent attack of coughing. 'Spit it out.'

'It's just that, what if there is nothing after this life?' I felt bad asking such a thing of a corgi who was not only my mentor, but who was himself seriously ill.

'Yes,' he nodded sagely. 'I suppose we all wonder this sometimes. But the energy we possess cannot be destroyed. It may change shape, but it has to go somewhere.' It was a while before he added, 'Like trapped wind.'

I was relieved Winston hadn't been upset by my indelicate question. 'Better out than in?'' I repeated his very personal liturgy. 'Winston's First Dictum?'

'Look sharp, dear boy,' he wheezed, humour lighting up his grizzled features as he spluttered in his basket. 'Watch how the most enlightened beings choose to spend their time. What do they hold to be important? That should give us a clue about life's greatest purpose.'

My thoughts turned immediately to Her Majesty, and how I owed her everything. If it hadn't been for her kind-heartedness and swift resolve, I wouldn't even be alive, let alone one of her canine representatives. I thought about Charles's work to reconnect people with the natural world and with each other – how eager he was for people to focus on what is meaningful. And the younger family members with their Royal Foundation. Each one of them, in their own way, spent a great deal of time and energy creating the causes for a happy mind – and, from the way Winston explained it, for a very great future happiness beyond this life.

When my thoughts turned back to myself, however, I felt uncomfortable. 'I know I'm still quite young,' I confessed to Winston. 'Barely out of puppyhood. But I wouldn't know where to start, you know, creating the true causes of a happy mind. You are a very wise corgi, you understand things. And Margaret –' I glanced in her direction '– she keeps things organised and shipshape. But I am a corgi with no special abilities. What can I do to help others?'

'Listen to your heart,' said Winston. 'It will become clear. You don't need any special ability to care for the well-being of others. Anyone can practise generosity, giving support to those around us. We all have plenty of opportunities to practise patience. The wonderful paradox is that the more we make the happiness of other beings our priority, the happier we become ourselves.'

I was following him closely.

Then very quietly, he added, 'But you are wrong to think you don't have a special ability that you will develop over time. It's a great relief for me to know that I can pass these particular duties onto you. You will inherit a sacred mantle that has been handed down, from one royal canine to the next, for the past thousand years.

I looked at Winston, uncomprehending. Special ability? Sacred mantle? What was he on about?

Blinking heavily, he observed my bewilderment. 'Think of my name, dear boy. That may give you a clue.'

'Winston,' I replied. '"We will fight them on the beaches."' I remembered very well the story about his willingness to defend his Queen against the onslaught of Rottweilers on a beach near Balmoral.

'And because they thought you liked cigars.'

A rueful smile crossed his face as he remembered. 'Yes, indeed. But there's another, more esoteric reason for my name.'

'Go on,' I urged him.

'Long before my namesake, Winston Churchill, became prime minister, he was a British soldier, fighting in South Africa. He was captured by the Boers, but managed to escape. In the darkness, he found his way to the only house in a thirty-mile radius which was sympathetic to the British cause. He was guided, dear boy. Intuition. Any other house, and he would have been recaptured and shot dead for trying to escape.'

My eyes were widening as I listened to this incredible tale.

'There were other occasions. Once he had to get into his ministerial car. A staff member held the door open for him. But instead, he stepped round to the opposite side of the vehicle and climbed in. During the journey, a bomb exploded on the side where he usually sat, blasting the car onto just two wheels. He told his wife later that an inner voice had directed him where to sit. Again, it was intuition that saved his life.

'This same ability was useful in helping others. Like the time he ordered all the staff at 10 Downing Street to evacuate the kitchen immediately. A short while later, the place was destroyed by an enemy bomb.'

It was the first time I had heard any of these stories. As I took them in, I wondered how they tied in with the reason for Winston's name – and with what he had said to me.

'That's amazing, Winston!' I said. 'Do you also have intuition?'

'Let's just say that I'm "sensitive",' he intoned this last word with great deliberation. 'As are you.'

'Me?!' In that moment, the only images that sprang to mind were of the embarrassing variety. Knowing my story as intimately as you do, my fellow subject, I'm sure there's no need for me to recite that litany of shame yet again.

'You don't think you came into this family by chance?' he challenged. He seemed to be suggesting a level of action behind my rescue from the Grimsleys – a subject I'd never even thought about, but which had my mind whirring.

'This intuition. Being sensitive,' I pressed him. 'How do you know I have it?'

Instead of replying, Winston succumbed to an attack of coughing, his whole body so wracked that the Queen got up from the Scrabble board and came over to the basket to re-assure him. It took the longest time for him to recover, the coughing subsiding to a deep gasping, before he was finally able to breathe more easily.

I turned, leaving him so that he could slip into much-needed rest. But despite the coughing spasm, he hadn't forgotten my question.

'All in good time, dear boy' he whispered, closing his eyes. 'We will speak before I go. But never forget: you are a divine creation of energy and consciousness. Understand this and you know what endures after this life ends.'

Winston's illness had a profound effect – and not only on me. He became the focus of the whole royal household, from the Queen down to the most junior footman – his every action monitored and the subject of discussion. Everything he ate – or didn't. His every lap of water. A short walk in the garden was now considered the most felicitous of events, suggesting that he wouldn't be leaving us just yet.

For the truth was that we had all come to realise that he would be leaving. Gone was all talk of a recovery. Instead, when Dr Munthe made his now less-frequent visits, all talk was of keeping Winston as comfortable as possible, increasing his pain medication to whatever was needed.

For increasing periods of time, Winston slept. When he did waken up, he'd slip in and out of normal consciousness, and everyone would watch him with deep concern because the coughing spells had become lengthier and more violent than ever. At the end of each one he seemed close to drowning, he was so short of breath. There were moments of horror when we'd all watch him struggle to take in air, his now more-frail body shuddering with the effort. Over the days he became less and less himself.

I had had plenty of time to reflect on our fireside conversation. In particular, Winston's observation about how the most enlightened people in our community focus on cultivating positive qualities of mind, rather than simply material well-being. The more audiences with Her Majesty on which I eavesdropped, the more I became convinced that this was true. The Queen herself was constantly emphasising the importance of inner qualities rather than outer trappings. Although I hadn't fully grasped why, before, now I began to understand – those same qualities were the true causes of happiness in life. And if what Winston said about consciousness was true, they would be the causes of happiness in the future too.

Little by little it dawned on me that there was a purpose to life. That we had the chance to use this precious existence to develop our most altruistic motives and compassionate instincts. To be the best that we could be!

As for that other part of the conversation, where Winston seemed to be saying I had some special ability, I put it down to the drugs. Nothing otherworldly had ever happened to me apart from the one encounter with Queen Elizabeth I – and that hadn't been in the least bit spooky. Even at the time of the encounter I had known there was something different about the presence of the first Queen Elizabeth compared to the second. But it hadn't felt as I imagined a psychic encounter to feel. There had been nothing supernatural about it. Neither the Queen, nor I, had left the royal library feeling in the least bit unsettled.

There can come a time, witnessing the decline of a loved one, when the peace of physical death starts to seem preferable to the torture of continued living. Winston spent most of each day asleep – the effect of the heavy medication Dr Munthe had prescribed for maximum comfort. During his rare moments of wakefulness, we all hoped he wouldn't succumb to an especially violent spasm of coughing. Following each of these we'd witness his agonising struggle for breath. One day, we all knew, he would no longer have the fight in him to survive.

It was late one afternoon in the Queen's private sitting room when he surfaced from the deep sleep in which he'd spent all morning. Her Majesty was downstairs giving an official audience and Margaret had accompanied her. So it was just the two of us in the soft, lamp-lit quietude. With the benefit of hindsight, I realised that this was just how Winston planned it.

I looked up as I saw him lift his head in his basket. This action alone took all his energy. His face now gaunt, his once-sleek coat lying lank, when he looked at me, there was still that spark of humour in his brown eyes.

'It's time,' he said simply.

'Oh, Winston!'

'For the best,' he gasped.

It took all my strength to retain my composure. 'You have been the most inspiring and wonderful mentor a corgi could ever have. I can never repay your kindness.'

Winston wheezed, before managing, 'I'm handing the bones over to you.'

'Yes.' I chose to agree with whatever would help him remain at peace.

After a period of laboured breathing he continued, 'Her Majesty's sensitive canine.'

'Well, I suppose I did see Elizabeth the First,' I said, somewhat surprised that he had returned to this unlikely subject.

'And the others.'

I cocked my head. I had no idea what he was talking about, but I didn't want to unsettle him.

He closed his eyes heavily and his head slumped in the basket. His breathing was slow, but regular, and I thought he must have drifted off to sleep. But after some time had passed, he murmured, 'The soldier on the stairs.'

I recalled the figure in chain mail who seldom seemed to move. How I'd been struck by the way that other members of the household paid him so little attention.

'You mean he's …'

'Yes. But not the main one.' At this point Winston began coughing. Fortunately, not deeply. But enough so that the rest of what he said was indecipherable. I gathered there was some other being who held a position of great significance, from whom I had much to learn.

Winston's spluttering subsided and his breathing became regular. Gentle. A sense of tranquillity came into the room, and even though it was late in the afternoon the light coming through the window changed in a way I would have found hard to imagine had I not experienced it for myself. It was as if we had been caught in a forest and had found our way to a clearing where the canopy above us had opened. We were illuminated in a light which had the clarity of dawn. Along with the light was an aroma I recognised, but couldn't immediately place: the aromatic fragrance of primordial woodlands.

'He's come to fetch me. As I live, so shall I die,' Winston said, quite clearly, before exhaling with a shudder.

I stared at him, knowing instinctively what had happened, but unable to believe or accept it. Willing him to breathe in again. But there was no movement in his body. Only the tranquil radiance of that clear light. A sensation of boundlessness which pervaded the whole room, and into which I knew that Winston was passing.

There was no time in that vivid brightness, as though it had been there all along, but I was only, for a short while, able to perceive it. Then the light began to fade.

I stared out the window. I will never know, my fellow subject, if what I saw was actually there, or only a figment of my imagination. But it seemed as if the clear light was being swiftly gathered into a figure who was standing directly outside, holding Winston in his arms. With his blue eyes, snowy white hair and moon-silver cloak, I instantly recognised Michael. And it suddenly occurred to me that he might be an angel.

Both he and Winston looked at me with expressions of the deepest love and reassurance. Then they dissolved rapidly upwards.

The sky was already darkening into evening. For the longest time, the last of that bright light remained, twinkling like a star in the canopy of nightfall. A gleaming reminder of the wisest dog I had ever known, and my dearest mentor. The one who had opened my eyes to mysteries and wonderment beyond anything I may have ever imagined. Hidden in plain sight.

Nine

Balmoral Estate, Scotland

It was our first summer holiday since Winston's death, and his presence had been missed by us all. How could we not trot into the drawing room, in the direction of that particular wing chair, without remembering Winston's triumphant vol-au-vents discovery? Or encounter a cluster of freshly disposed cigar stubs without our thoughts turning to our wise and faithful friend?

The times I missed him most were when we were together as a family. In particular, going for walks on those long, Scottish evenings, far into the countryside or deep into the forests, while savouring the lingering softness of heather, or feeling the crackle of autumn leaves beneath our paws – I would recollect my first experience of these vivid sensations and how Winston had been there by my side.

On one such evening, Charles, William and Harry took Margaret and me as they walked through a forest on the estate. We set out in a Land Rover, William behind the wheel, driving some way off-road before getting out of the vehicle and making our way into the forest.

The trees were mysterious in the dusk and paths pungent with the scent of deer as we set off, single file. The men didn't speak much, taking the opportunity to walk among rocks clad with the thickest moss, and alongside rushing streams without the need for conversation.

At one point Charles, who was leading, paused and pointed. Through the dark limbs of trees we spotted a herd of red deer. Upwind of us, they hadn't noticed our approach. At least not to begin with. William looked at Margaret and me and made a cautioning gesture, before moving forward in silence and stealth.

We corgis may be very close to the ground, but over the next few minutes we crept so near to the herd that even we could make out their individual shapes. In particular, a stag who was the closest to us, his massive antlers and heavy mane silhouetted in the twilight. We all watched as he and some of the does raised their heads, noses sniffing the air, for the first time suspecting a presence. The stag turned, facing us directly, still unable to see us, but growing wary. It seemed hard to believe he couldn't make us out, so distinct were his features, even to the fleck of silver in his eyes. Then he had turned his neck and was gesturing the herd to move away, not in alarm, but with clear intent.

We paused, watching them vanish into the woods, their departure as silent as our approach had been.

'The woods are lovely, dark and deep,' I remembered Winston once murmuring in this same forest. Ah, Winston, I thought, as we stood, motionless. How much pleasure he would have taken in that encounter with the red deer.

We continued on for a short distance, coming to a spot where there were several large boulders among the trees at the right sort of height to be used as seats.

Charles eased onto one of them while his sons paused beside him, William producing a bottle of water out of his pocket, from which they took it in turns to sip.

Looking up at where the pines soared towards a copper sky, William was the first to speak. 'Always great to be back in the forests.'

'Very therapeutic,' agreed Charles.

'Much easier to forget all about ...' Harry made a gesture signifying London and the constant pressures of living in the royal goldfish bowl.

'Exactly,' his father agreed. 'Here it's just us, and nature. No appointments diary.'

Harry was nodding. 'Whenever I'm in nature – doesn't matter if it's Scotland or somewhere in Africa – I wish I could spend more time out here.'

'Yes,' agreed Charles. 'Strange to think how, for hundreds of thousands of years, most people's lives revolved completely around the cycle of the seasons. Now there are children who think that milk and eggs come from factories.'

'All the more reason to get people into the wild,' said Harry.

As the three of them pondered this for a while, I snuffled around the stones behind them, scuffing away a layer of pine needles with my paw and taking in the earthy aroma beneath.

'I heard it suggested the other day,' said Charles, 'that we don't so much come into nature, as come out of it.'

I looked at where he was sitting pensively, and immediately thought of Winston. This was exactly the kind of enigmatic pronouncement he might have made.

William tilted his head, questioningly.

'The idea being,' continued Charles, 'that even though we feel quite separate from nature, we are entirely a product of it. Our body is ninety per cent water, all of which ultimately comes from natural sources. We are completely dependent on oxygen, produced by the trees. And we need food, which, in the end, all comes from the soil. Plus we depend on the sun's heat, for our body temperature, and to grow crops. So we are, in fact, an entirely natural product derived from air, water, earth and heat.'

'The four elements,' observed William.

Harry was nodding.

While Margaret inspected the forest floor, I returned to the group, wagging my stump.

'I suppose even Nelson doesn't come into nature, so much as out of it,' said Harry, bending to pat me.

The other two looked at me for a while before William commented, 'I think our little friend is missing Winston.'

'As are we all,' agreed Charles after a while.

I felt less alone when he said this, and walking over to him, I nuzzled his ankle with my nose.

'He was a remarkable little chap, Winston,' said Charles. 'And I have a feeling that Nelson here is going to be remarkable too.'

Aware that others in the family were feeling Winston's loss may have deepened my own moments of melancholy, had it not been for a piece of wisdom which was as entirely unexpected as it was life-changing.

Several evenings later, I joined Her Majesty as she took a brief stroll outside before retiring for the night. We had had a quiet and uneventful evening after an equally quiet and uneventful day. Far from the usual busyness of royal life, we had spent most of our time relaxing together - just the family. For that very reason, perhaps, Winston's absence could not have been more strongly felt.

Standing on the lawn, the Queen's eyes were drawn to the satin sky which, in this remote part of her realm, was utterly dark, providing the perfect backdrop for every constellation to twinkle with unlikely radiance, and for a perfectly full moon, which lit the landscape in ethereal silver.

The Queen stood, taking everything in for a few moments before she turned to look at me. 'We all miss dear Winston,' she said, as though summarising my own sentiments for much of the past few days. 'But wherever he is, I have no doubt that his wisdom and cheerfulness will be serving him very well.'

I took a few steps towards her.

'In the meantime, you and I have to make the most of our own precious life. When we go back to England, I expect that in due course we will be joined by another corgi. Perhaps several others.'

There had been talk of this between Her Majesty and Lady Tara, so the idea didn't come as a complete surprise. I immediately found myself wondering if any of the new royal corgis would include one as wise and companionable as Winston. Before deciding, only moments later, that they almost certainly would not.

'There will never be another Winston,' the Queen continued. 'Nor should we try to recreate the past. Instead, this is your opportunity to lead our newcomers in the ways and rituals of royal life, to share the wisdom that Winston shared with you.'

I leaned against her leg. It was an extraordinary idea that I should be like Winston. And who was I to try?

'We never feel ready,' she continued seemingly able to read my thoughts. 'I was only 25 when I was crowned. Do you think I felt fully prepared? Somehow, with support from others, we work things out. Anyway, little one –' she leaned down to pat my neck '– you have come far. You already know more than most about purpose.'

As the Queen and I shared that moonlit Scottish night, I contemplated what she had just said.

In my earliest days in the royal household, and directly at the feet of Her Majesty, I had learned the importance of not being preoccupied by appearances. Just because someone had a floppy ear, or wanted to become a wildlife photographer instead of an investment banker, didn't render him unlovable – or deserving only of a one-way trip to the shed.

From Her Majesty's horse trainers I had heard how impulse control is critical if we are to cultivate the habits of success. Only when we are able to delay gratification can we hope to fulfil our most heartfelt wishes, or highest purpose.

From the Archbishop of Canterbury, whose leg had been such an embarrassing provocation, I had come to know that the extrinsic trappings of affluence are less important to our happiness than the intrinsic things – like the communities we live in, the people that we care about us, the activities that connect us to others.

The positive dog trainer had revealed the importance of not only of consistency, but also of being authentic. Self-doubt, and other inner battles, may be so much a part of us that they have become part of our physical being – but we can learn to let go of them. There is no need to be permanently defined by our past.

From Michael I had come to understand how we can only experience the most transcendent states of consciousness by embarking on an inner journey. How we all have the opportunity to practise alchemy – to turn the base metal of our lives into pure gold. How the material world is much less solid than it appears, because it is also energy – and that energy is no other than our own consciousness.

Winston had been the repository of a great many insights: how young people were the best source of canapés at any royal event; how hiding things in plain sight was remarkably effective – everyone being so caught up in their own thoughts that they hardly noticed. It was Winston who had shown me the difference between merely knowing something, and having it change one's behaviour – at which point it matured into wisdom. Most profoundly, he had been the one to make clear that we shouldn't shy away from thoughts about death. Quite the opposite. It was very important to keep focused on what we take with us – not jewels and trinkets, but our state of mind: cultivating the true causes of a happy mind being something we energise by giving happiness to others.

And how would I ever forget Winston's First Dictum – better out than in?

As for the Queen, she was a living, breathing example that a fulfilled and purposeful life arises when we use whatever abilities we have for the greater good. Do small things with great love. And, what I'd learned from her only moments ago: that it's unwise to wait until we're completely ready – because we may never be.

I remembered the conversation with Winston when he'd told me he was handing down his particular duties, a sacred mantle that had been passed from one royal canine to the next for the past thousand years. And what he'd said, just moments before his death, about handing over the bones to me. Now the Queen herself was urging me to take on his role.

From very close by came the hooting of an owl in an other-worldly invocation, before the bird revealed itself for just a few moments, diving from a nearby fir tree, gliding across the lawn and into the woods. The rare sighting made this moment with Her Majesty feel even more mysterious and special.

The Queen looked down at me. 'The sun, the moon and the truth cannot be hidden. How fortunate for us all, Nelson, that you came to our family. Everything for a reason.'

I met her gaze with deep adoration, my stump wagging appreciatively – how else could I show her that was exactly how I felt too?

The Braemar Gathering, held on the first Saturday of September, has been a uniquely Scottish tradition for many hundreds of years, and one attended by the British monarch for well over a century. Scottish sports like tossing the caber and putting the stone were part of the occasion, but the festivities included Highland dancing and piping events.

The informality of the gathering makes it an occasion suitable for royal corgis to attend. Which was how, one Saturday morning found Margaret and me in the back of a Range Rover with Her Majesty, heading to nearby Braemar. As was often the case, Her Majesty's private secretary, Julian, occupied the passenger seat, and ran through the day's events as we made our way through the glorious Scottish country-side. I was far more interested in the passing scenery than in VIPs and protocols, so I paid very little attention to what he was saying. Until he mentioned St George's School.

I had forgotten about how Her Majesty had asked to include the school at the Braemar Gathering, after the bullying incident at Buckingham Palace. But it was all coming back to me – and I was now most curious to watch the St George's School bagpipe band, under Jenkins's leadership.

Then Julian broke the news. 'Apparently they're not able to perform, ma'am.'

'Really?' replied the Queen, in a tone of voice that demanded further explanation.

'No reason was given.'

'Travel problems?' she probed.

'They arrived yesterday. Members of the band have been seen at Braemar, in uniform. I received a text message from their headmistress, Miss Thwaites, a short while ago.'

'Have you replied?'

'No, ma'am. Only just got it.'

Her Majesty looked pensive for a few moments before she told him, 'Tell Miss Thwaites that I am looking forward *greatly* to seeing the St George's school band perform.'

'Yes, ma'am.' Julian was already fiddling with his phone. If he was in any way surprised by her direction, he wasn't showing it.

I looked across the back seat at Her Majesty curiously. I wondered if I could detect a certain gleam in her eye.

I had already been to a couple of gatherings in the past and discovered they were quite unlike most other events that the royal family attended. As well as the competitive atmosphere on the sports field, there was an informality about the games, almost a sense of family about them, with the different clans dressed in their various tartans. As we royal corgis accompanied our family around the grounds that day, there were ceremonies and presentations but there was also a palpable pride in coming together as Scots, giving the day its special flavour.

After Julian had reminded us of the St George's school bagpipe band that morning, my main interest had been in their appearance. If, indeed, they did appear. I wondered why it was they had told him that they couldn't? Why Her Majesty had responded in her unusual way? I found myself caught up with a sense of growing anticipation.

And so no one was more interested than me when it was announced that the massed bands event was about to start. I pricked my one and a half ears up very keenly.

A great phalanx of kilted men carrying pipes and drums was forming on the fields before us. Literally hundreds of them coming together in tartans of every hue. Many of them were seasoned veterans of the gatherings, having attended this special day, as men and boys, for generations. There was a sprinkling of younger faces. And then I noticed, at the very front, a small pipe band of youngsters. In the front row, at the very centre, a noticeable gap.

As the final bands lined up at the back of the massed column, a silence descended, before the announcement was made that the event would be led by the band of St George's School, appearing at the specific invitation of Her Majesty the Queen.

Following the announcement, the sense of expectation greater still. Everyone focused on the school group at the head of the group – and in particular, on the space at the centre of the very front row. If this was a theatrical ruse, designed to grab our attention, it was working well. As each second ticked by, the feeling of suspense deepened.

Knowing of the exchange in the car earlier that morning, I wondered if the Queen's message had propelled the English visitors into an appearance that was about to unravel in the most embarrassingly public way.

As the whole Scottish nation waited – or so it felt – and still, there was no sign of the school band's leader, the uncertainty grew to unbearable levels.

Until finally, there was a movement, and from behind the front row, and into the centre, arrived the boy I recognised as Jenkins. From a distance it was hard to see the expression on his face, although there did seem a pallor I didn't remember from before. Raising the mouthpiece of his pipes to his lips, amid that great silence he stepped forward and began to play, in solo, the first, evocative lines of 'Amazing Grace'.

After only two lines of the melody, there was a movement behind him, and from the front row stepped another boy who accompanied him for the rest of the verse. Lanky and bespectacled, I didn't recognise him at first. It took the Queen herself to jolt my memory as she leaned over to her private secretary, Julian, and asked him, 'Is that Simpson?'

Checking his program, he nodded.

'Much taller,' observed Her Majesty.

After a verse, the soloists were joined by the rest of their band, and very soon, by all the bands, who then began marching in slow procession.

There are, my fellow subject, few experiences as rousing as the massed bands of Scotland marching across green,

September fields, in a display of the most ancient sounds and symbols of that rugged Celtic land. All became drawn into the music and spectacle of a ritual which, at a level deeper than words, is a moving reminder of a special heritage.

The bands made their way slowly across the fields, and passed where the royal family stood to watch. Compelling as the clansmen were, there was one particular group – in fact, two particular performers – which held Her Majesty's attention. And focused as they were on the way ahead, both Jenkins and Simpson couldn't avoid a sideways glance at the royal party and where the Queen watched with a smile.

It was only later, when the massed band recital had come to an end, that the mystery of that morning's message to Julian was solved. The Queen requested Jenkins and Simpson to be brought to the VIP area. Huchens himself ushered them into the royal presence. I noted how both of them bowed and greeted her as Your Majesty as though they had been practising.

Stepping apart from others in the group, the Queen looked from one to the other of them. Jenkins looked somewhat less pale than he had earlier, but there was still a certain peakiness about his appearance. Simpson bore only a passing resemblance to the boy we had met earlier in the year, having benefited from a growth spurt that had propelled him upwards.

'It was a great surprise to see not just the one of you, but both of you,' observed Her Majesty.

'Jenkins has been teaching me the bagpipes,' explained Simpson, his bass voice cracking sharply into falsetto on the word 'bagpipes'.

'It was nice of you, Jenkins, to share your solo.'

'Thank you, ma'am,' Jenkins glanced somewhat nervous-ly at Simpson.

'Earlier today, someone told you that you might not be appearing.'

'Yes, ma'am.' Simpson nodded.

Jenkins was looking at his feet, flecks of pink appearing on his neck and cheeks.

When neither of them volunteered an explanation, she persisted. 'I do hope no one was ill?'

'No, ma'am,' offered Simpson.

'Not exactly,' said Jenkins.

The two looked at each other briefly before Jenkins ad-mitted, 'I got a bit nervous, ma'am.'

'I see.'

'Very nervous,' he confessed.

'Oh, dear.'

'I was throwing up in the toilets,' he told her, encouraged by her sympathy.

'It was coming out both ends,' added Simpson.

'How interesting,' said the Queen in a tone of voice which commanded that this particular line of conversation be dropped instantly. 'But you made a recovery.'

Jenkins nodded, 'It was Simpson who did it, actually.'

Her Majesty fiddled with the strap of her handbag, 'Good for you, Simpson. A few words of encouragement?'

'Yes, ma'am. I told him to imagine everyone in the audi-ence as naked, 13-year-old freshers who he was about to turn the fire hose on.' His voice was modulating wildly. 'It seemed to perk him up.'

Jenkins was nodding vigorously.

'Reframing technique,' explained Simpson, shoving his heavy glasses back up his nose with his index finger.

If the Queen was in any way startled by this information, she wasn't showing it. 'I gather your studies have progressed smoothly?' she asked Simpson.

'Yes, ma'am. Thank you. I have been accepted by Oxford.'

'Well, good luck with your history degree.'

'Actually, psychology.'

Her Majesty pursed her lips. 'Didn't you learn the names of all the kings and queens of Britain since 1066?'

'Yes, ma'am. I had to learn something to prove a memory technique.'

'I see.' The Queen looked philosophical for a while before saying, 'I have a feeling that psychology is going to suit you very well indeed.'

'Thank you, ma'am.'

Later that day at Balmoral, drinks were being served in the drawing room. And vol-au-vent canapés to accompany them – including several plates with lobster fillings. The weather had continued to be simply glorious, and with only family, dear friends, and closest members of the household present, it was the happily relaxed end to another Braemar Gathering.

In one corner, Kate, William and Harry were playing with George and Charlotte, while Charles and Camilla looked on. Her Majesty was making her way towards them when Lady Tara approached her with an apprehensive expression,

'I know this is somewhat short notice, but I was wondering if I could have some time away next weekend.'

'Of course, my dear.' The Queen didn't hesitate. 'We'll still be on holiday.'

'Oh, good!' Tara seemed relieved. 'I'm planning a week-end break.'

'Barcelona?' asked Her Majesty.

Tara nodded. 'Richard asked me again, and I thought ...'

'Very good.' The Queen smiled brightly. 'He changed his mobile ... thingummy then?'

Tara shook her head. 'I changed my attitude.'

'Even better,' nodded the Queen.

Over with the children, Harry was regaling the group with a story about how, earlier in the day, an ancient Highlander had tried to teach him how to recite the first verse of a Robbie Burns poem. Kate explained how she had also been the focus of instruction, with a Scots lady encouraging her to learn the steps of a Highland Dance, which she demonstrated to the amusement of all.

Charles looked up at his mother. 'Were you taught any-thing today, Mummy?' he asked, jokingly.

'As a matter of fact, I was,' replied Her Majesty. 'A young man almost let nerves get the better of him today. His school friend gave him some advice I don't think I'll ever forget.'

As her whole family watched her, intrigued, the Queen seemed to turn into Andrew Simpson, lanky and bespectacled, her whole posture and demeanour changing. 'Imagine everyone in the audience as naked, 13-year-old freshers,' she mimicked Simpson, her voice breaking from bass into falsetto. 'And you're about to turn the fire hose on them'.

Everyone laughed.

'You'll have to remember that next time you open Parliament,' suggested Harry.

'What an appalling image!' said Charles.

'Or confronted by the media scrum,' offered William.

Listening to the conversation on a nearby sofa, Philip seemed about to say something. Muscles of his jaw clenched and lips quivering as though forming the letter 'b', he seemed to be about to express himself, before thinking better of it, and sinking back into his seat.

Observing his father closely, Charles followed up on what William had just said. 'They seem to have left us alone this summer.'

'That's because of all the baby photos we let them take earlier in the year,' suggested William.

'Long may it continue,' said the Queen to general agreement.

'Looks like the corgis are off the hook, then,' Charles looked down at where I was sitting next to his mother. 'Didn't you have the idea, Harry, of offering them up for a photo-shoot.'

'A few years ago,' Harry agreed.

'That's right,' said William, turning to his grandmother. 'You were even going to ask Nelson to write something meaningful.'

'Kate thought he had it in him to produce a whole book,' Harry reminded them.

'Indeed,' said the Queen, meeting my eyes with a twinkle. 'I wouldn't be surprised if he hasn't done exactly that.'

Read the Prologue and
Chapter One of

The Dalai
Lama's Cat

Prologue

The idea came about one sunny Himalaya morning. There I was, lying in my usual spot on the broad, first floor windowsill, the perfect vantage from which to maintain maximum surveillance with minimum effort, as His Holiness was bringing a private audience to a close.

I'm far too discreet to mention who the audience was with, except to say that she's a very famous Hollywood actress ... you know the one married to the equally famous actor, who played husband and wife undercover agents in that thriller a few years ago? The actress who does the refugee charity work – yes, *her*!

It was as she was turning to leave the room that she glanced out the window, with its magnificent view towards the snow-capped mountains, and noticed me for the first time.

'Oh! How adorable!' she stepped over to stroke my neck, which I acknowledged with a wide yawn and tremulous stretch of the front paws. 'I didn't know you had a cat!' she exclaimed.

I am always surprised how many people make this observation – though not all are as bold as the American actress in giving voice to their astonishment. Why should His Holiness *not* have a cat – if, indeed, 'having a cat' is a correct understanding of the relationship, a subject to which we will return later. It is not as if people are required to tell everyone they meet about the companions with whom they share their lives. How many people do you pass in the street wearing the lapel badge 'Cat haver?'

Exactly.

Besides, those with particularly acute observation would know of the feline presence in His Holiness's life by the stray hairs and occasional whisker I make it my business to leave on his person. Should you ever have the privilege of getting very close to the Dalai Lama, and scrutinise his robes in detail, you will almost certainly discover the finest wisp of white fur, confirming that, far from living alone, he shares his inner sanctum with a feline of impeccable – if undocumented – breeding.

It was exactly this discovery to which the Queen's corgis reacted with such vigour when he visited Buckingham Palace – an incident to which the World Media were strangely oblivious.

But I digress.

Having stroked my neck, the American actress, asked, 'Does she have a name?'

'Oh yes! Many names,' His Holiness smiled enigmatically.

What the Dalai Lama said was true. Like many domestic cats I have acquired a variety of names, some of them used frequently, others less so. One of them, in particular, is a name I don't much care for. Known among His Holiness's staff as my ordination name, it isn't a name the Dalai Lama himself has ever used – not the full version, at least. Nor is it a name I will disclose so long as I live. Not in this book at least.

Well … *definitely* not in this chapter.

'If only she could speak,' continued the actress, 'I'm sure she'd have such wisdom to share.'

And so the seed was planted.

In the months that followed I watched His Holiness working on a new book, the many hours he spent making sure texts were correctly interpreted, the great time and care he took to ensure that every word he wrote conveyed the greatest possible meaning and benefit. More and more I began to think that perhaps the time had come for me to turn my paws to a book of my own – a book that would convey some of the wisdom I've learned sitting not at the feet, but even closer, on the very lap of the Dalai Lama. One that tells my own tale – not so much one of rags to riches as trash to temple. How I was rescued from a fate too grisly to contemplate, to become constant companion to a man who is not only one of the world's greatest spiritual leaders and a Nobel Peace Prize laureate, but who is also a dab hand with the can opener.

Often in the late afternoon, after I feel His Holiness has already spent too many hours at his desk, I will hop off the wooden sill and pad over to where he is working, rubbing my furry body about his legs. If this doesn't get his attention I sink my teeth, politely but precisely, into the tender flesh of his ankles. That always does it.

With a sigh, the Dalai Lama will push back his chair, scoop me up into his arms, and walk over to the window. Looking into my big, blue eyes, the expression in his own is one of such immense love that it never ceases to fill me with happiness.

'My little bodhi*catt*va,' he will sometimes say playfully, calling me by one of my many names. In the Tibetan Buddhist path, 'bodhisattva' refers to an enlightened being.

Together we gaze out at the panoramic vista that sweeps as far as the eye can see down the KangraValley. Through the open windows a gentle breeze carries fragrances of pine, Himalayan oak and rhododendron, giving the air its pristine, almost magical quality. Held in the warm embrace of the Dalai Lama, it as though all distinctions dissolve away completely – between the observers and the observed, between cat and lama, between the stillness of twilight and the bountiful appreciation of my deep-throated purr.

It in those moments that I feel profoundly grateful to be the Dalai Lama's cat.

Chapter One

I have a defecating bullock to thank for the event that was to change my very young life – and without which, dear reader, you would not be holding this book.

Picture a typical monsoonal afternoon in New Delhi. The Dalai Lama is on his way home from a teaching trip to the USA. Having recently arrived at IndiraGandhiAirport his car is making its way through the outskirts of the city when traffic is brought to a halt by a bullock that has ambled into the centre of the highway where it proceeds to dump copiously on the tarmac.

Several cars back from the fray and unable to see the cause of the traffic jam, unlike many of those in the vehicles around him, His Holiness did not join in the chorus of raised voices and angry gesticulations, but took the opportunity to abide calmly in the present moment. As he did, his attention was drawn to the drama being played out at the side of the road.

Among the usual seething clamour of pedestrians and bi-cyclers, of food-stall holders and beggars, two ragged street urchins were anxious to bring their day's trading to an end. Earlier that morning, they had come across a litter of kit-tens, concealed behind a pile of hessian sacks in a back al-ley. Scrutinising their discovery closely, they soon realised that they had fallen upon something of value. For the kittens were no common or garden variety moggies, but a rather superior kind altogether. The young boys were unfamiliar with the Himalayan breed, but they recognised in the handsome colouring, the sapphire eyes and the lavish pelt, a tradeable commodity.

Rough handing us from the nest in which our mother had tended to us, they thrust my siblings and I into the terrifying commotion of the street. Within moments, my two eldest sisters, who were much the larger and most developed of us, had been exchanged for rupees – an event of such excitement that I was dropped, fell painfully onto the ground and only narrowly avoiding being killed by a deafening scooter.

The boys had had much more trouble selling us two younger kittens, our features being less developed, our eyes barely open. For several hours they trudged the streets, shoving us vigorously at the windows of passing cars. Much too young to be taken from our mother, my small body was simply unable to cope. Failing fast for lack of milk, and still in pain from tumbling to the ground, I was barely conscious when the boys sparked the interest of an elderly passer by, who had been thinking about a kitten for his grand-daughter.

Gesturing to put us two remaining kittens on the ground, he squatted on his haunches and inspected us closely. My older brother padded across the corrugated dirt at the side of the road, mewing imploringly for milk. When I was prodded from behind to induce some movement, I managed only a single, lurching step forward before collapsing painfully into a puddle of mud.

It was exactly this scene that His Holiness witnessed.

And the one that followed.

A sale price agreed, my brother was handed over to the toothless old man. I, meantime, was left mired in the filth while the two boys debated what to do with me, one of them shoving me roughly with his big toe. They decided I was unsaleable. Fate sealed, they grabbed a week old Sports page of the India Times that had blown into a nearby gutter, and wrapped me like a piece of rotten meat to be discarded in the nearest rubbish heap.

As I began to suffocate inside the newspaper, the light of life inside me flickered low. Every breath became a struggle. I was about to be snuffed out.

Except that His Holiness despatched his attendant first. Having just got off the plane from America, the Dalai Lama's attendant happened to have two, single dollar notes secured within his robes. He handed these over to the boys who scampered away, speculating with great excitement about how much the dollar bills would fetch when converted into rupees.

Don't lose sight of those two ragamuffins as they dance away through the puddles, for we will meet them later – in rather different circumstances.

Unwrapped from the ignominy of the Sports pages ('Bangalore Crush Rajasthan By 9 Wickets'), a short while later I was resting in comfort in the back of the Dalai Lama's car with milk being dripped into my mouth as His Holiness willed life back into my limp form.

I remember none of the details of my rescue, but the story has been recounted so many times that I know it by heart. What I do remember is waking up in a sanctuary of such infinite warmth that for the first time in my young life I wanted to see all that I could. As I did, I found myself looking directly into the eyes of the Dalai Lama.

How do I describe the first moment that you find your-self in the presence of His Holiness?

It is as much a feeling, as a thought. An intuitive under-standing, deeply heart-warming and profound, that all is well. It is as though for the first time you become aware that your own true nature is one of boundless love and compassion. It has been there all along, but the Dalai Lama sees it and reflects it back to you. He perceives your Buddha nature, and this ex-traordinary revelation often moves people to tears.

In my own case, swaddled in a piece of maroon-coloured fleece on a chair in his office, I was also aware of another im-portant fact. A fact that is of the greatest importance to all cats and for which we all have an awareness that comes as a standard feature of our in-built cat nav; I was in the home of a Cat Lover.

As strongly as I sensed this, I was also aware of another, less sympathetic presence across the coffee table. Back in Dharamsala, His Holiness had resumed his schedule of audi-ences immediately, and was fulfilling a long standing commit-ment to be interviewed by a visiting history professor from Britain. I couldn't possibly tell you who, exactly, just to say that he came from one of England's two main ivy league uni-versities, you know the ones that take part in that boat race every year, the team flying the dark blue colours. Yes – *them*.

The professor was penning a tome on Indo-Tibetan his-tory and seemed irked to find he was not the exclusive focus of the Dalai Lama's attention.

'A stray?' he exclaimed after His Holiness briefly explained the reason why I was occupying the seat between them.

'Yes,' confirmed the Dalai Lama, before responding not so much to what the visitor had said, as to the tone of voice in which he'd said it. Regarding the history professor with a kindly smile, he spoke in that rich, warm baritone with which I was to become so familiar,

'You know, professor, this stray kitten and you have one very important thing in common.'

'I can't imagine,' responded the other, coolly.

'Your life is the most important thing in the world to you,' said His Holiness. 'Same for this kitten.'

From the pause that followed, it was evident that for all his erudition, it was the first time the professor had ever been presented with such a startling idea.

'Surely you're not saying that the life of a human and an animal are of the same value?'

'As humans we have much greater potential for development, of course. But the way in which we all want so very much to stay alive, the way we cling to our particular experience of consciousness – in *this* respect human and animal are equal.'

'Well, perhaps some of the more complex mammals ...' the professor was battling against this troubling thought, 'but not all animals. I mean, for instance, not *cockroaches*.'

'Including cockroaches,' His Holiness was undeterred. 'Any being that has consciousness-'

'But they carry filth and disease. We *have* to spray them.'

His Holiness rose and, walking over to his desk, lifted up a large match box. 'Our cockroach carrier,' he said. 'Much better than spraying. I am sure,' he delivered his trademark chuckle, '*you* wouldn't want to be chased by a giant, who sprays you with toxic gas.'

The professor received the truth of this self-evident, but uncommon wisdom, in silence.

'For all of us who have consciousness-' the Dalai Lama returned to his seat, '-our life is very precious. For this reason we need to protect all sentient beings as much as possible. Also, we should recognise that we share the same two basic wishes: the wish to enjoy happiness, and the wish to avoid suffering.'

They were themes I have heard the Dalai Lama repeat often when he meets people, and in limitless ways. Yet every time he speaks with such vivid clarity and impact it is as though he is saying them for the first time.

'We not only share these wishes. Even the way we seek out happiness and try to avoid discomfort is identical. Who among us does not enjoy a delicious meal? Who does not wish to sleep in a safe, comfortable bed? Stray kitten, author or monk – we are all equal in that regard.'

Across the coffee table, the history professor shifted in his seat.

'Most of all,' the Dalai Lama leaned over me and stroked me with his index finger, 'all of us just want to be loved.'

By the time the professor left, later that afternoon, he had a lot more to think about than his tape-recording of the Dalai Lama's views on Indo-Tibetan history. His Holiness's message was challenging. Confronting, even. But it wasn't one that could be easily dismissed ... as we were to discover.

In the days that followed I became quickly familiar with my new surroundings. The cosy nest His Holiness created for me out of an old, fleece robe. The changing light in his rooms as the sun rose, passed over us, and set each day. The tenderness with which he fed me warm milk until I was strong enough to begin eating solid food.

I also began exploring. First, the Dalai Lama's own suite. Then out beyond it, to an office shared by his two Executive Assistants. One of them, the young, roly-poly one closest the door with the smiling face and soft hands was a monk called Chogyal who helped His Holiness with all monastic affairs. The older, tall one, who sat opposite, always in a dapper suit, and whose hands always had the clean, tang of carbolic soap was a trained diplomat called Tenzin. He assisted on secular matters.

That first day I wobbled round the corner into their office, there was an abrupt halt in the conversation.

'Who is this?' Tenzin wanted to know.

Chogyal chuckled as he lifted me up and put me on his desk, where my eye was immediately caught by the bright blue top of a Bic. 'The Dalai Lama rescued her while driving out of Delhi,' Chogyal repeated the attendant's story as I flicked the Bic top across his desk.

'Why does she walk so strangely?' the other wanted to know.

'Apparently she was dropped on her back.'

'Hmm,' Tenzin sounded doubtful as he leaned forward, scrutinising me closely. 'Perhaps she was malnourished, being the smallest kitten. Does she have a name?'

'No.' Then after a short period flicking the pastic pen top to and fro, 'We'll have to give her one!' he was enthusiastic about the challenge. 'An ordination name. What do you think – Tibetan or English?'

In Tibetan Buddhism, when someone becomes a monk or nun they are given an ordination name to mark their new identity.

Chogyal began suggesting different possibilities before Tenzin suggested, 'It's better not to force these things. I'm sure something will present itself as we get to know her better.'

As usual, Tenzin's advice was both wise and prophetic – unfortunately for me, as things turned out. Chasing the biro top, I progressed from Chogyal's desk half way across Tenzin's before the older man seized my small, fluffy form and put me down on a runner.

'You'd better go down,' he said. 'I have a letter here from His Holiness to The Pope and we don't want paw prints all over it.'

Chogyal laughed, 'Signed on his behalf by His Holiness's Cat.'

'HHC,' Tenzin gave the abbreviated version. In official correspondence, His Holiness is frequently referred to as HHDL. 'That can be her provisional title until we find a suitable name.'

Beyond the office of his personal assistants was a corridor that led past further offices towards a door that was carefully closed behind anyone who arrived or left. I knew that door led to many places including Downstairs, Outside, The Temple and even Overseas. It was the door through which all His Holiness's visitors came and went. It led to a whole new world. But in those early days, as a very small kitten, I was perfectly content to remain on this side of it.

Having spent my first days on earth in a back alley, I had no understanding of human life – and to begin with, nor did I have any idea how unusual my new circumstances were. I watched the way that visitors always presented His Holiness with a white scarf or katag (pronounced 'carter') and how he returned it to them with a blessing. Was that not the way that humans usually behaved when they met?

When he got out of bed at 3 am every morning to meditate for five hours, I would follow him, curling in a tight knot beside him, glowing in his warmth and energy. Was this not the way that most people started each day? I was also aware that many people who visited him had travelled very long distances to do so – that all seemed perfectly normal to me too.

Until one day Chogyal picked me up in his arms and tickled my neck. 'Who are all these people?' he followed my gaze to the many framed photographs on the wall. 'They are the past eight Presidents of the United States meeting His Holiness. He is a very special person, you know.'

I did know. He always made sure my milk was warm, but not too hot, before giving it to me.

'He is one of the world's greatest spiritual leaders. We believe he is a living Buddha. You obviously have a very close karmic connection to him. It would be most interesting to know what that is.'

A few days afterwards, I found my way down the corridor to the small kitchen and sitting area, about half way down the corridor, where the Dalai Lama's staff would relax, have their lunch and make tea. Several monks were sitting on a sofa, watching a recorded news item on his recent visit to USA. By now they all knew who I was – in fact I had become the office mascot. Hopping up on the lap of one of them, I allowed him to stroke me as I watched TV.

All I could see, initially, was a vast crowd of people with a tiny red dot in the centre, while His Holiness's voice could be heard quite clearly. But as the news item progressed I realised that the red dot *was* His Holiness, in the centre of a vast, indoor sporting arena. It was a scene that was replayed in every city he visited from New York to San Francisco. The newsreader commented how the huge crowds of people that came out to see him in every city showed that he was more popular than many rock stars.

Little by little I began to realise just how extraordinary the Dalai Lama was, and how highly regarded he was by human beings. By extension, it seemed to me that I must be rather special too. It was me, after all, who he had rescued from the gutters of New Delhi. Had he recognised in me a kindred spirit – a sentient being on the same spiritual wave length as him?

When I heard him tell visitors about the importance of loving kindness, I would purr contentedly, certain in the knowledge that this was exactly what I thought too. When he opened my evening can of Snappy Tom's, it seemed as obvious to me, as it was to him, that all sentient beings wanted to fulfil the same basic needs. And as he stroked by bulging tummy afterwards, it seemed equally clear that each of us just wanted to be loved.

There had been some talk around this time about what would happen when His Holiness left on a three week trip to Australia and New Zealand. With this, and many subsequent travels planned, should I remain in the Dalai Lama's quarters or would it be better if I was found a new home.

New home? The very idea of it was crazy! I was HHC, with an established position in the establishment. You might say I had become part of the smooth running of the place. Had not Tenzin himself said that the Dalai Lama and I had a *close karmic connection*?

Then one day it happened. His Holiness was over at the temple, and The Door was left open. By then I had grown into an adventurous kitten, no longer content to spend all her time cosseted in fleece. Prowling along the corridor in search of excitement, the moment I saw the door ajar, I knew I had to go through it, to explore the many places to which it led.

Downstairs. Outside. Overseas.

Somehow I made my shaky way down two flights of stairs, grateful for the carpeting as my descent accelerated out of control and I landed in an undignified bundle. Picking myself up, I continued across a short hallway and outside.

It was the first time I'd been outdoors since being mired in the gutters of New Delhi – there was a bustle, an energy, with people walking in every direction. I hadn't got very far before I heard a chorus of high pitched squealing and the commotion of many feet on the pavement. A tour group of Japanese school girls caught sight of me and took pursuit.

I panicked. Racing as fast as my unsteady hind legs would take me, I lurched away from the shrieking hoard. I could hear them gaining ground. There was no way I could out-run them. The leather of their shoes on the pavement became a thunder!

Then I spotted the small gap. It was between bricks that led under the building. A tight squeeze. And very little time. Plus I had no idea where it led.

But as I bolted inside, the pandemonium came to an end. I found myself in a large, low space between the ground and the wooden boards of a veranda floor. It was dark and dusty and there was a constant, dull drumming traffic of feet above. But at least I felt safe. I wondered how long I would need to stay there until the schoolgirls had gone away. Brushing a cob-web from my face, I didn't want to risk another such ordeal.

As my eyes and ears adjusted to this new place, I became aware of a scratching noise. Sporadic, but insistent bursts of gnawing. I paused, nostrils flared as I searched the air.

Yes! The aroma was unmistakeable. Along with the sound of incisors came a pungent whiff that set my whiskers tingling. The reaction was instant, powerful, and instinctive: the scent of mouse!

I moved, stealthily, in the direction from which it was coming. Downwind of the creature, my approach was con-cealed beneath the constant sound of footfall.

Even though I had never seen a mouse in my life before, I recognised what it was immediately. Holding onto a vertical foundation strut, its head was half buried in a wooden beam which it was hollowing out with its large front teeth.

Instinct took over.

With a single swipe of my front paw I swept the rodent off balance and onto the ground where it lay stunned. Reaching down I sank my teeth into its neck. The body went limp.

I knew exactly what I must do next. Prey secured, I pad-ded back to the gap in the wall, checked the pavement traffic outside. Finding no Japanese schoolchildren, I hurried back into the building. Across the hallway. Up the stairs. To The Door – which was firmly closed.

I had to remain there for quite some time until one of His Holiness's staff arrived. Recognising me, but without noticing the trophy in my mouth, he let me in. I padded down the cor-ridor and around the corner.

Because the Dalai Lama was still at the temple, I made my way directly into the office of his Executive Assistants, announcing my arrival with a meow of all due urgency and importance.

Responding to the unfamiliar tone, Chogyal and Tenzin both turned, looking at me in surprise as I strutted proudly into their office and deposited the mouse on the carpet.

Their reaction was nothing like I had expected. Exchanging a sharp glance, they both instantly moved from their chairs, Chogyal lifting me up and Tenzin kneeling down over the motionless mouse.

'Still breathing,' he said. 'Probably in shock.'

The printer box,' Chogyal directed him to an empty cardboard box from which he'd just removed a fresh cartridge.

Using an old envelope as a brush, Tenzin soon had the mouse in the empty container. He regarded it closely. 'Where do you think-?'

'This one has cobwebs on its whiskers,' observed Chogyal.

This one?

It?!

At that moment, the Dalai Lama's driver arrived in the office. Tenzin handed over the box with instructions that the mouse was to be observed and, if it recovered, released in the forest nearby.

'HHC must have got out,' observed the driver meeting my blue-eyed gaze.

Chogyal was still holding me, not in his usual affectionate embrace, but as though restraining a savage beast.

'HHC. I'm not sure about that title anymore,' he said.

'It was only a provisional title,' concurred Tenzin, returning to his desk. 'But His Holiness's Mouser doesn't seem appropriate.'

Chogyal put me back on the carpet.

'What about just 'Mouser' for an ordination name?' suggested the driver – but because of his strong, Tibetan accent, it came out 'Mousie.'

All three men were now looking at me intently. The conversation had taken a dangerous turn which I have come to regret ever since.

'You can't have just 'Mousie,' said Chogyal. 'It has to be Something Mousie or Mousie Something.'

'Mousie Monster?' contributed Tenzin.

'Mousie Slayer?' suggested Chogyal.

It was a pause before the driver came out with it. What was to become my ordination name. The name that is my deepest regret. The name that dare not be spoken.

'What about Mousie-Tung?' he suggested.

All three men burst out laughing as they looked down at my small, fluffy form.

Tenzin turned mock-serious as he regarded me directly, 'Compassion is all very well. But do you think His Holiness should be sharing his quarters with Mousie-Tung?'

'Or leaving Mousie-Tung in charge for three weeks when he visits Australia?' mused Chogyal.

Getting up, I stalked from the room, ears pressed back firmly and tail slashing.

In the hours that followed, as I sat in the tranquil sunlight of His Holiness's window, I began to realise the full enormity of what I'd done. For almost all of my young life I had sat listening to the Dalai Lama talk about how the lives of all sentient beings are as important to them as our own life is to us.

But how much attention had I paid to that on the one and only occasion I was in the real world?

His Holiness often repeated the truth that all beings wish for happiness and to avoid suffering. A thought that hadn't crossed my mind when I'd stalked the mouse. Not for one moment had I considered my actions from the *mouse's* point of view.

I was beginning to realise that just because an idea is very simple, doesn't make it easy to follow. Also, that purring in agreement with high sounding principles actually means nothing if you don't actually live by them.

I wondered if His Holiness would be told the new 'ordination name' – the grim reminder of the greatest failing of my young life. Even worse, would he be so horrified when he heard what had happened that he would banish me from this beautiful haven forever?

Fortunately for me, the mouse recovered and was released into the forest. And when His Holiness returned, he was immediately caught up in a series of meetings.

It wasn't until late in the evening that he mentioned the subject. He had been sitting up in bed reading, before closing his book, removing his glasses, and placing both on a bedside table.

'They told me about what happened,' he murmured, reaching over to where I was dozing nearby. 'Sometimes our instinct, our negative conditioning can be over-powering. Later we come to regret what we have done. But that is no reason to give up on yourself – the Buddhas haven't given up on you. Instead, learn from your mistake and move on.'

He turned out the bedside light, and as we both lay there in the darkness, I purred gently in appreciation.

'Tomorrow we start again,' he said.

The next day, His Holiness was going through those fortunate few pieces of mail that his Executive Assistants selected for his attention from sackfuls that arrived every morning.

'This is very nice,' he turned to Chogyal, holding up a letter and accompanying book that had been sent as a gift by the professor of history from England.

'Yes, Your Holiness,' Chogyal studied the glossy cover of the book.

'Not so much the book,' said His Holiness, 'as the letter.'

'Oh?'

'After thinking about our conversation, the professor says he has stopped using snail bait on his roses. Instead, he now releases the snails over the garden wall.'

'Very good!' smiled Chogyal.

'We liked meeting him, didn't we?' he glanced up at me directly.

I remembered how, at the time, I'd thought how deeply unenlightened the professor had seemed. But after what had happened the day before, I could hardly judge.

'Just shows that we all have the capacity to change,' the Dalai Lama twinkled. 'Doesn't it, Mousie?'

About the Author

David Michie is the internationally best-selling author of a *The Dalai Lama's Cat* series, as well as the non-fiction titles *Why Mindfulness is Better than Chocolate*, *Hurry Up and Meditate* and *Buddhism for Busy People*. His books are available in 25 languages and over 30 countries.

David is a regular keynote speaker at major conferences. He delivers mindfulness and meditation seminars and courses to a diverse range of audiences. In 2015 he established Mindful Safaris to Africa, combining game viewing and meditation sessions in journeys to unexplored places, outer and inner.

David grew up in Zimbabwe, a place teeming with African wildlife, but home was always with his corgi Tudor, who had an ear that, instead of standing, flopped.

For more about his work, go to: www.davidmichie.com

72775739R00138

Made in the USA
Lexington, KY
03 December 2017